Stages Of A Woman

A Collection Of Short Stories

By
J. J. Caldwell

PublishAmerica
Baltimore

Grateful acknowledgment is made for permission granted to reprint all or excerpts from the following copyrighted materials:

There's A Hole In My Bucket
By Michael Lloyd, Carol Rosenstein & Bruce Gowers, employees of Together Again Productions, Inc. © 1987
Permission granted by Together Again Video Productions.

For Once In My Life
Words by Ronald Miller
Music by Orlando Murden
© 1965 (Renewed 1993) JOBETE MUSIC CO., INC. and STONE DIAMOND MUSIC CORP.
All Rights Controlled and Administered by EMI APRIL MUSIC INC. and EMI BLACKWOOD MUSIC INC.
All Rights Reserved International Copyright Secured Used by permission.

Back Cover photo by Claire Heath of Claire Photography, www.clairephotography.com. Copyright 2003.

ISBN: 1-59286-997-1
PUBLISHED BY PUBLISHAMERICA, LLLP
www.publishamerica.com
Baltimore

Printed in the United States of America

This book is a work of fiction.

Names, characters, places, and incidents are either the product of the author's imagination or are used fictitiously. Any references to real events, businesses, organizations, and locales are intended only to give the fiction a sense of reality and authenticity. Any resemblance to actual events, locales, or persons - living or dead - is entirely coincidental.

To my girl, Chundra.
You've known me when... you know me now, thanks for being a true friend, having my back i caring about me just because I'm me. Love ya, Mitai

♀ <u>Dedication</u> ♀

I humbly dedicate this book to my Creator and Guide; the One who is my everything.

Thank You, God. Thank you, for all you have done for me, for all that You are doing through me, and for all that You have brought me through.

I know with You, all things are possible. You have shown me that dreams really can come true! You have blessed me with this opportunity to speak to the world, so I am giving this book back to You.

♀ <u>Acknowledgments</u> ♀

I would like to personally and lovingly acknowledge those in my life whose support and influence caused this book to "be."

My mother, Gloria J. Hearne – Thank you for giving me life and for all of your support, especially during the roughest times and transitions of my becoming the woman that I am today.

My father, the late Richard J. Caldwell Sr. – Thank you for loving me and for teaching me not to worry about what other people think of me, or allow them to hold me back from my destiny.

My big brother, Addis Jerome – Thank you for being there for me while growing up and for teaching me how to read and write. Without you, this book wouldn't be possible.

My big sister, Esther – Thank you for all of the pushes and pep talks, as you encouraged me to find my niche and follow my dreams.

My son and personal assistant, Ri'chard – You are my angel, my motivation to reach higher, to go farther and to keep on trying, even when I feel like quitting. You have been such a big help in getting this book together.

My love, my friend, and my encourager, Mark G. – Thank you for believing in me and my writing, supporting me through stressful moments, constantly reminding me that I belong to God and all that I do should glorify Him.

To the rest of my family and friends – Singling out each one of you would be another book by itself! Thank you all for your love and support, I love you dearly!

♀ INTRODUCTION ♀

After many bouts of discouragement, lack of confidence, focus, and motivation – not to mention writer's block – I have created this collection of short stories entitled *Stages Of A Woman*. As I see it, it is a miracle from God that others will now read what I have worked on, worried about, and prayed over during the past six years. A writer can only write about what he or she knows, whether they have learned from personal experiences or research and observation. So, for me to get to the point where I felt comfortable enough to open up my heart and mind to be exposed and scrutinized by others has taken some time.

There are many different messages present within these stories. It is my hope that you will find the message that is meant for you and that *Stages Of A Woman* will come across as more than just a couple of entertaining stories. It is my fervent prayer that these stories can also encourage others toward positive thoughts, actions, and life directions. The characters – more often than not –realize that God is present in their struggles, He has the answer to their problems, and I sincerely hope that you – my reader–will realize this within your own life as well.

I don't ever this want book to be pigeonholed as only an "African-American" book, written only for African-American women. This book is for all women, of all races, cultures, and nationalities. *Stages Of A Woman* deals with issues that have crossed color lines and gender lines; it goes into the head and the heart. This book is written especially for the women who wake up every morning and put on their "masks" to hide their pain, going out onto the "stage" of life, constantly pretending that everything is perfect in their world, day in and day out. It is for these nameless "masked" actresses that I humbly tell their stories to the world, so that they may never have to "unmask" to know that they are not alone in their struggles.

When I first began writing *Stages Of A Woman* in 1997, I was dealing with some tough personal issues. I began to unburden my soul in the best way that I knew how at the time, by writing. I let these words pour from my broken heart and confused mind, releasing all of the built-up pressure that was inside of me. I didn't know it at the time, but I was on my own personal spiritual journey to becoming a woman.

Stages Of A Woman is a collection of short stories about women at different stages of their lives, tales of their trauma and trials. Each of these individual women within *Stages Of A Woman* have bumped their heads by taking in many wrong ideas that have been ingrained into their minds by society, authority figures, and their own selfish and personal desires. In one-way or another they have allowed others to dictate – if only for a brief moment– what love, happiness, and life should be all about. It is my hope that women of all races can relate in some way to these stories, because ultimately, we are all women. We all cry, dream, laugh, love, get hurt by others and hurt ourselves at times as we journey through life.

I want to thank you for supporting my work and for taking the time to "listen" to my voice. May God bless you and keep you.

Enjoy!

Peace and Blessings,

J. J. Caldwell

TABLE OF CONTENTS

♀   ♀

PART I

~ GROWING UP

I was born
So now I'm here
But I didn't know
That I would shed so many tears!

♀   ♀

# THERE WAS A HOLE IN MY BUCKET

Willie: There's a hole in my bucket, dear Liza...
Liza: Then, mend the hole, dear Willie...
Willie: With what shall I mend it, dear Liza?
Liza: With a straw, dear Willie...
Willie: But the straw is too long, dear Liza...
Liza: Cut the straw then, dear Willie...
Willie: With what shall I cut it, dear Liza?
Liza: With a knife, dear Willie...
Willie: The knife is too dull, dear Liza...
Liza: Whet the knife then, dear Willie...
Willie: With what will I whet it, dear Liza?
Liza: With a stone, dear Willie...
Willie: But the stone is too rough, dear Liza...
Liza: Smooth the stone then, dear Willie...
Willie: With what shall I smooth it, dear Liza?
Liza: With water, dear Willie...
Willie: In what shall I carry it, dear Liza?
Liza: In a bucket, dear Willie...
Willie: But there's a hole in my bucket, dear Liza!

(There's A Hole In My Bucket)

♀ <u>Verse One – The Cause</u> ♀

"There's a hole 'n my bucket…"

I really like singin' that song. It's my favorite. My big brother, Michael, he always sings that song to me at night. That's how I learned it. I like skippin' rope to it, too. It even makes me feel better when I start to get sad.

Grownups say, "Ava, chile, you need to smile more. You used to smile a lot; why you don't no more? You're too young and pretty to be so sad and serious."

I really am sad a whole lot though, so I don't smile. Don't want to. They think because I'm only six years old I shouldn't have too much to be sad about. But they don't know about Mister Phil – he's my first-grade teacher. He teaches us a lot of things. We learn all about letters, colors, numbers, and shapes. My favorite shape is a square, and I can count all the way to one hundred all by myself!

I really used to like goin' to school. I used to think he was a really nice man, Mister Phil. He would give me candy, and he told me I was the cutest little girl he'd ever met, and that I had the *prettiest* curly hair he'd ever seen. He said I was his most favorite and smartest student. He gave me lots of attention and he always made me feel special. I told him I wanted to be a teacher just like him when I grow up, and he said I could practice by helpin' him out.

Mister Phil would let me stay in the classroom with him at recess time. He'd let me clean the chalkboards, grade papers, and do anythin' else that real teachers got to do. It was fun too…for a while. I used to like stayin' in the class with him by myself until…, well, until he started to touch me in places that Mommy said nobody should touch me.

The first time it happened, I was really scared. I started to cry and told him to stop. But he didn't. I told him I was gonna tell my mommy. Mister Phil just laughed at me and then started talkin' to me in a real mean and scary way. He said if I ever told my mommy or anybody, he would say I was lyin'. He said because he was a grown-up everybody would believe him, and they would think I was a bad girl and a liar. He said he'd tell Mommy I was a nasty girl, and that I went behind the portables to play bad games with the little boys if I ever told her about what he was doin' to me.

I wasn't a bad or nasty girl, but what he said scared me, and I didn't want to be lied-on or get in trouble. I really didn't like it when Mommy whupped me. What if he was right and Mommy wouldn't believe me? What if nobody would ever believe me? I decided I couldn't, shouldn't, and wouldn't tell. Anybody. Ever.

Mister Phil kept on touchin' me more and more, almost everyday. He started to send notes home sayin' that I had done this or that bad thing in class so that I would have to stay late after school the next day. Every time I had to get Mommy to sign those notes I would want to cry. I wanted to scream and tell the world, "Mister Phil isn't nice! He touches me in bad places and sometimes he even makes me do nasty things to him! I hate him!"

I got a lot of whuppins behind his lies, which made me believe even more that I couldn't and shouldn't ever tell. His lies were stronger than my truth. So, I never said a word. I figured that if I just closed my eyes hard enough and if I pretended long enough, it would all become just a part of my imagination -Mister Phil, the touchin', and all of the bad feelin's that I had on the inside. Everything would just go away.

But like Willie in the song, there's a hole in my bucket and the truth keeps drippin' out, no matter what I do. I'm always so sad because I have nightmares, too; about Mister Phil. But I'll just keep tryin' harder, and pretty soon, it'll all just go away. If I just keep tryin' to make it a big make-believe story, one day, it won't be real anymore. Yeah, that'll be nice. That's what I want.

♀ <u>Verse Two – The Effect</u> ♀

"There's still a hole in my bucket…"

Hey, it's me again, Ava. I'm halfway grown now! Thirteen years old, finally a teenager! Everything in the world seems so different and confusin' now. One minute, I just *know* that I know way more than Mommy ever did, and the next minute, I'm not sure about one single thing! My body is changin' and my face is changin', but on the inside I still feel like little six-year-old Ava, and I don't know why.

For some reason, I'm scared of grown men. Teachers, preachers, policemen; if they're a male, I just don't like 'em and I don't trust 'em. Every time Michael asks me why I don't like this man or that man, all I can say is, "I just don't!"

You know what else? I don't like myself much either nowadays. The other kids call me weird and ugly and I think they're right. I don't talk much or participate in any activities unless I have to. I'm really skinny but I try to hide myself with big baggy clothes – so no one can see my body– but I can't hide my face. Wish that I were a turtle so that I could hide in my shell forever! I really don't know why I hate myself so much.

Maybe it's a phase, like Mommy says. All I know is that I want to die. Literally. I just haven't been successful with any of my suicide attempts. Yet. I really feel like "endin' it all" when those horrible feelin's rise up from deep inside of me, when I feel anxious and scared, when I feel so vulnerable and alone, totally unprotected! I just don't quite know what I feel the need to be protected from.

In English class yesterday, we had to do vocabulary words. We had a list of twenty words and had to look up their definitions in the dictionary. When I got to the definition of word number seventeen, I felt physically ill. I wanted to vomit and run out of the class – and as far away from the school as I could go -

and never look back.

Those bad feelin's came out again, but this time they went wild! I felt an inescapable suffocatin' fear and the need to flee or fight to protect myself. I had never heard the word before – pedophile – and after readin' it's meaning, I vaguely remembered someone who possibly did somethin' horrible to me. I had convinced myself it was all a dream, but if that was truly the case, then why was I reactin' so harshly? Like somethin' really had happened to me?

Why's there this voice – soft and scared – whisperin' in my head that the *imaginary* Mister Phil is real and that he did indeed hurt me years ago? I don't understand and, honestly, I don't want to. I don't want to know, feel, or think of *anything* that has to do with the imaginary Mister Phil. So, if I close my eyes hard enough and if I pray to God long enough, these horrible feelin's and thoughts will go away.

But I'm afraid that there's a hole in my bucket, because as hard as I try to suppress these thoughts and deny these terrible feelin's and as much as I ignore the possibility that someone harmed me long ago, I keep havin' the same nightmares that I've been havin' since I was six years old. The nightmares about a Mister Phil.

♀ <u>Verse Three – The Truth</u> ♀

"There's yet a bigger hole in my bucket..."

Once more, I'm back! I've gotten through those rotten teenage years and have truly come into my own. I'm *grown*, twenty-two, gorgeous, sassy, and nothin' and nobody can hold me back! I'm in the process of findin' myself and exactly what I want out of life, and as far as I'm concerned, this world is my toy!

Me and my best friend Nicole, we got some serious plans of becomin' big time stars. Singers, models, actresses, either one, it don't matter. Well, let me rephrase that. We *had* some plans...until she up and got married on me. She just had her baby and I'm on my way over there to see the little rug rat.

Oh, no! I'm here at Nicole's front door and I can already hear the baby cryin'! I'm in *no* way ready for nobody's kids...

Hold up! Who's that comin' up here? I *know* he don't think nobody wants to see him! It's Nicole's ex-stepfather, Josh. Nicole's mother divorced his sorry butt a few years back when she found out that he was molestin' Nicole. Nicole was real messed up behind it, too. That sick pervert, he just keeps comin' around, like he's still family!

Uh-oh! Now here comes Rashawn, Nicole's husband, and he's headed straight for Josh. By the look on Rashawn's face, there's gon' be *big* trouble. Let me move out of the way, find my girl, and make sure she's okay.

This is strange; why's this room so dark?

"Nicole...Nicole? Girl, what's wrong? You okay? Yeah, I saw his sorry butt out there. Rashawn gon' handle it, though. Awh, don't cry, girl. Everything's all right now. Josh won't hurt you like that ever again."

Hold on...wait a minute. Somethin' is wrong; somethin' in me feels *way* wrong, like somethin' is breakin' inside of me.

This seems so familiar to me – her pain. Her words, I've never said them, but I've lived them a thousand times over…in those horrific nightmares.

OH, GOD, NO! IT WAS REAL. IT DID HAPPEN! There is a Mister Phil, and he did hurt me!

"Nicole, I gotta go! Yeah, I'm okay, I'm fine, I just gotta go!"

I gotta get out of here, gotta find Mommy and I gotta tell her what Mister Phil did to me!

Well, I finally did it. I told Mommy what happened. Part of me is still a bit scared, still wonderin' if it all really happened or if I got false memories planted by some made-for-television movie, like they talk about on the news.

Mommy took the news like a champ; she took me in her arms and comforted me as I cried and told her my darkest secret. She didn't ask me why I waited so long to tell her. She just held me, listened to me, believed me, and let me know that everything would be all right.

What happened next shocked me and hurt me more than I could've ever imagined. Mommy went to find Mister Phil. She and Uncle Jake found him, pinned him against the wall in his own living room, put a pistol to his head…then, he admitted every single thing that he had done to me. He *admitted* it! It was true!

With his admission, I had to finally face the fact that I had been molested. I had to face all of the pain, fear, and guilt that I had been avoidin' and ignorin'. I had to deal with every single feelin' that came along with his violation of my body. I could no longer suppress or deny the thoughts and images of his abuse; he verified that it had really happened. It was real, not some figment of my imagination, not some terrible nightmare as I had desperately hoped.

I wanted to curl up and hide under a rock, never to see the light of day again. Anything would've been better and easier to do than to deal with all of the feelin's that I had goin' on inside of me. It was too much, too fast; I couldn't handle it on my own. I couldn't close my eyes tight enough to make it all go away. I couldn't wish or pretend anymore that nothin' had ever happened. I didn't know what to do.

Mommy wanted me to press charges against Mister Phil, but I couldn't bring myself to relive that time and tell total strangers of my deepest shame. But it turned out that Mister Phil had made a habit out of molestin' little boys and girls; a few of his other former students stepped up with their stories to ensure that Mister Phil got locked away for a long time. And Mommy got me some help.

♀ <u>Verse Four – The Healing</u>♀

"There *was* a hole in my bucket…"

Yep, I remember that crazy song from a long time ago. It always made me laugh because the guy with the hole in his bucket, Willie, was in a mess of a situation. No matter what, he couldn't get past the fact that there was a hole in his bucket. No matter what suggestions he was given by Liza to fix his problem, he just ended up back at Square One.

In my mind, Willie was doomed, hopeless, and above all *stupid*. That's what made it so funny. To me, Willie was one of those people that the old folks would classify as "can't get right." Now– with the knowledge I have – after all I've been through and all of the counselin' I've received, I know that Willie wasn't stupid nor doomed unless he chose to be. He was in fact hopeless, and didn't see that he could and should abandon that old bucket and get a new one. Willie had a one-track mind and couldn't or wouldn't change his way of thinkin', even if it were to his own detriment.

How can I be so judgmental? How do *I know* this? True enough, I'm no expert psychologist who can pick apart the mind of imaginary folk song characters. I'm just a thirty-year-old woman who can relate to Willie.

The reason that I know so much is because, like Willie, there was "a hole in my bucket," my mental, emotional, and spiritual "bucket," better known as my soul. That hole was punched in my bucket when I was molested at the age of six. It was a quite a hole, too. It was small enough for my young mind to cover up and keep a dark secret for years, but it was large enough for the little life force that I had at the time to seep through.

As I grew, the hole grew bigger, allowin' any self-esteem I was to grow into through my adolescent years to drip, drip, drip out– waterin' worries, doubt, self-hatred, and suicidal thoughts –

instead of nourishin' my inner most parts.

But like I said, there *was* a hole in my bucket. Ava Nichelle Barnes has overcome, healed, and is stronger because of an event that the devil had sent my way to weaken and ultimately destroy me. In all of his arrogance, the devil didn't think that God would bring me through. But He did.

My therapist– a true angel – talked to me about some guy named Freud. She explained that my reaction to the molestation was called a defense mechanism. She said I had gone into denial and that my nightmares were due to what's known as repression. My young mind pushed hard, but those painful thoughts and feelin's that I was tryin' to keep so neatly locked away just kept tryin' to make their way out into my conscious.

She told me what happened that day at Nicole's house was the "trigger" that caused a repression breakdown, causin' me to let down my defenses and face the hard truth. She also talked to me about my faith in God, the fallacy of man, and forgiveness. She said that I would be a better and stronger woman when I learned to forgive Mister Phil for what he had done.

Forgive him? I told her that it would be a cold day in *Hell* before I forgave that perverted monster! But she was patient and continued to work with me. Eventually, I came to understand what she was tryin' to teach me. Until I allowed myself to forgive him, to let go of my anger for what he had done to me, and until I relinquished my right to blame and punish him, I would always be his victim even when he was dead and gone. Eventually, I realized that until I could forgive him: one, God wouldn't forgive me of my sins; and two, I would always have the nightmares, the pain, and the fear. I knew that I had a choice to make. I had to choose to take back my life and move forward or forever be little six-year-old Ava masqueradin' around in an adult body.

After a year and a half of weekly therapy sessions, I was able to forgive Mister Phil. Don't get me wrong; he and I will *never* be "cool." I may be healed, but I'm not crazy! That man is a habitual sex offender and has some serious issues. Forgiveness and trust are two different things, and I'll never trust him. If Mister Phil *ever* gets out of jail and tries to come near me, oh, believe me, he will regret it!

Unlike some survivors of sexual abuse, I don't feel the need to confront or accuse him, to show him how "strong" I am. I no longer feel anger toward him or fear of him. As a matter of fact, I don't feel sorry for him, either.

What do I feel? I feel free. Free to be me; I feel powerful and in control. In control of all of me, my life, heart, mind, and body. I no longer choose to be a victim; I choose to be, and most certainly am, victorious. I've let go of all of my "survival" techniques – all of the ineffective ways that I used to cope with my painful past.

I've chosen to be an overcomer of past sexual abuse, not just a survivor. See here, you can survive just about anything; the real work is in overcomin' an issue. I know that all of this strength has come from God, and I thank Him for bringin' me through. Just look at what He did… there was a hole in my "bucket," but He blessed with a brand new one. And you know what? God can do the same for you.

FINALLY A FAMILY

F

Cheyenne

"So, what name did you come up with?"

"I named her Kenosha Ann Collins, Momma," Cheyenne hesitantly replied to her mother's question. Cheyenne felt relieved that her mother was on the other end of the phone – and not in her face – when she told her what she had named her daughter. "Are you gonna come see her?" she asked in a hopeful voice.

"What? Cheyenne, you didn't like the name I picked out for it?" Vivian asked with a mixture of disbelief and disgust.

Cheyenne cringed at the tone of her mother's voice and the fact that she had just referred to her beautiful baby girl as "it." She also noticed that her mother had ignored the invitation to see the baby. Cheyenne knew in her heart her mother wasn't going to step foot in the hospital to visit either one of them.

She sighed heavily and said, "Momma, I have to go. The nurse is here with the baby. I need to feed her."

"Humph, then I *guess* I'll call you later!" huffed Vivian.

Cheyenne put the receiver down gently. She felt guilty for lying to her mother – the baby was sound asleep next to her – but she couldn't take her mother's attitude. She had enough to deal with experiencing postpartum depression; her emotions were running wild and she felt totally out of control. Not to mention adjusting to waking up in the wee hours of the morning to breastfeed a newborn.

Cheyenne decided that her mother's moodiness was just too much for her, and she wouldn't deal with anything that she could avoid. She wasn't good at standing up to her overbearing mother, so avoidance was her only option.

Cheyenne recalled how she had desperately tried to keep her marriage to Kenneth a secret, but eventually her mother found out – and she was livid. Cheyenne was quite aware that her mother didn't like Kenneth – she never pretended to like him, either – and Cheyenne knew why. But for the life of her, she couldn't understand why her mother wouldn't just accept the fact that her "baby" was grown and in love with a man that she had picked for herself.

Kenneth wasn't perfect, but he was the man that Cheyenne had chosen. Still, he didn't meet her mother's standards. Cheyenne reminded herself that her mother was probably just lonely and jealous. Her mother had been very bitter since Cheyenne's father had left to be with another woman. It didn't help things much when they all found out the woman he had left her mother for was White. One would think that race wouldn't be an issue – being Vivian was half-White herself – but let Vivian tell it; it was different, totally different.

Vivian had thrown a fit when she found out that Cheyenne and Kenneth were having a baby. She begged, cried, and pleaded with Cheyenne to have a miscarriage, an abortion, or to put the child up for adoption. She told Cheyenne to just do *anything* but bring that man's child into her family. Vivian said that she didn't want *her* daughter impregnated by "that low-life Kenneth Collins."

Cheyenne believed that her mother's hatred toward Kenneth had a lot to do with his dark skin color and the low opinion her mother held toward anyone who couldn't pass the "brown bag" test. Cheyenne figured her mother really didn't want her to have the baby out of fear that the child would be of a dark complexion – like Kenneth.

Momma really has some serious color issues left over from her childhood, she thought. Cheyenne remembered all of the stories that her mother had shared with her about "those hateful Black kids" who used to tease and pick on her because of her color. Her mother said she had vowed to never befriend or marry a "darkie," – the term she used for all dark-skinned people– she didn't want "them" around her, and definitely didn't want any of "them" in her family.

"Oh well, Kenosha, looks like she didn't get her wish, 'cause here you are, huh, Gorgeous?" Cheyenne said as she cuddled the sleeping mahogany-brown newborn. "Let's see…when you opened your eyes, I saw that they were green like mine and it already looks like you're gonna have a lot of wavy hair like me too. You know what, sweetie? You look like a brown version of Mommy! Guess now we need to give you a nickname, somethin' that's as cute as you are. Ummm, let me think. Ke-Ke; yeah, that's it, Ke-Ke. Sleep well, my precious angel." Cheyenne kissed the baby's hair and nestled the little one close to her body as she dozed off.

Vivian

Vivian slammed the receiver down and cracked the base of the phone. "I can't believe her! So stupid! So naïve! I know I taught her better! Isn't that right, Pookie?"

"Awk, right!" answered Vivian's pet parrot.

"Of all of the men on this earth, Cheyenne just had to go get herself mixed up with some low-life, a common hood. And he's black as night to boot! That boy ain't nothin' but a two-bit hustler who claims he's gon' make it big in the music business. Hmph, from what I see, the only way he's gon' make it big is by sellin' all of the stereos that he be stealin' out of folks' cars!

"Cheyenne thinks I'm stupid, like I don't know nothin'. People talk and they tell me things. And now he done got my daughter pregnant and as sure as my name is Vivian Marie Alexander, he's just gon' leave *us* to raise that baby of his!" Vivian ranted as she paced the floor. "But I ain't gon' do it! You know what, Pookie? I don't like him, I don't like that baby of his, and I never will!"

"Never will." repeated the parrot.

A

Cheyenne

"Awh, girl, don't trip off yo' momma. You *know* how she is!" Heather said as she walked to the bathroom to get some tissue for Cheyenne, who was crying hysterically. "S-s-he could have at l-l-e-ast called to say that she wasn't comin' to Ke-Ke's birthday party! E-ev-ery year it seems like it's the same thing over and over." Cheyenne cried as she grabbed the tissue from her best friend's hand.

"My momma acts so funny-style about Ke-Ke. You know, Papa, Trevon's son? Well, when it was *his* birthday, Momma went all out! She nearly bought out the entire toy store for him! She's always favored Papa over Ke-Ke and doesn't mind lettin' the world know of her preference either. I know it's because he's light-skinned!

"Heather, a grandmother just ain't supposed to act like that, showin' partiality and actin' ugly! It ain't right! Ke-Ke is six now and gettin' to the age that she can see and understand that she's bein' treated different. You know how smart she is," Cheyenne said as she blew her nose on a wad of tissue.

"Girl," Heather said, "like I told you, don't worry about it. What goes around comes around, and one day yo' Momma is gon' need Ke-Ke. Mark my words. It's karma, girl, karma."

Heather hugged Cheyenne as Ke-Ke came into the room.

"Hi, Mommy. Is Grandma Vivian comin' to my birthday party? I made her a special picture. See?" Ke-Ke handed her mother a picture of a yellow flower drawn on pink construction paper. Cheyenne smiled through her tears. Ke-Ke had put a lot of effort into the drawing; she had even stayed within the lines.

"This is really nice, Baby. Uh, no, sweetie, Grandma won't be able to make it today. She isn't feeling too good." Cheyenne felt pangs of guilt pinch her heart for the lie that she had just told her daughter. She hated lying to her, but it was the only way she felt she could protect her from the truth. Cheyenne wondered how much longer she would be able to keep the truth about her mother's feelings toward Ke-Ke a secret.

"Awh! She never comes to my parties! When she has a party, I'm not goin' neither!" Ke-Ke pouted and stomped out of the room.

Cheyenne and Heather looked at each other.

"Yep, looks like she's figurin' things out, all right," Heather sighed.

"I know," replied Cheyenne, "It's my hope that my momma comes around. This has gone on long enough. Regardless of anything, we're all family and we all got the same blood."

"True, true. So, are you gonna confront her about the way she treats Ke-Ke?" Heather asked.

Cheyenne took a deep breath and looked up at the ceiling. "Been there, tried that. She just denies it and has all kinds of justifications and excuses. Now, I just try to ignore her ways. Shoot, instead of being a caterer, my momma should've been a lawyer!"

The two giggled as they got up to finish decorating the house for Ke-Ke's birthday party.

Vivian

"Gon' ask me if I was comin' to that girl's party. Hmph, I got too many important things to do than to go to some ol' birthday party. I got clothes to wash, furniture to dust; in a few hours, my favorite TV show is comin' on. I can't miss that!" Vivian talked out loud to herself as she began gathering up her clothes to wash.

"See, I was right! I told Cheyenne that Kenneth wasn't no good. A mother knows these things; you just can't trust them dark men. I wasn't shocked at all when he ran off with one of the neighbors, leavin' Cheyenne with that baby. But I refuse to pick up his slack and take care of that child. I told Cheyenne not to have that baby! Wantin' me to come by some party. She knows I don't like that child. Ke-Ke, hmph! I guess that's short for 'monkey,' 'cause Lord knows that little Black girl looks like one!"

Vivian laughed at her own cruel joke. She picked up her hamper of dirty clothes and told her parrot Pookie, "I still don't like that girl and don't want nothin' to do with her. And I ain't never goin' to no stupid party for her either!"

The parrot ignored Vivian as it ate its food.

M
Ke-Ke

"Ke-Ke, I want you to take this plate over to your Grandma Vivian's house for me," Cheyenne said as she handed her daughter a plate piled with food.

"Uh, Ma, I didn't come home for spring break to see that old woman. Why can't you take it over there? Or better yet, why don't she just come by and pick it up herself?" Ke-Ke retorted with a voice full of attitude. "She ain't never liked me no way; why should I break my neck doin' anything for her?" she asked her mother.

"Oh, chile, you know your Grandma Vivian is old and gettin' sickly nowadays, and old folks are real stuck in their ways. Sometimes, you gotta just learn to let some people be how they gon' be! Now, I'm not askin' you, I'm tellin' you to take this plate over to your Grandma's house!" Cheyenne said in a tone that let Ke-Ke know she wasn't playing around and that she meant business.

"All right, I'm goin'. Where are the keys to your car?" Ke-Ke asked in a huff.

"Right there, on the table. Don't you be huffin' at me, Missy. Nineteen ain't too old to get a whuppin!" her mother warned. "And make sure you bundle up 'cause it's still kinda cold out there. I been watchin' how you been dressed lately, in them flimsy clothes. Bein' cold ain't cute, girl!" Cheyenne joked, hoping to make Ke-Ke smile.

Ke-Ke playfully rolled her eyes at her mother as she grabbed the car keys and dinner plate from the table, and grudgingly went out to deliver the food to her Grandma Vivian.

Vivian

When she heard a car pulling into her driveway, Vivian peeked through her curtains to see who it was. At first she thought it was Cheyenne coming to see her, but when she saw Ke-Ke getting out of the car, she groaned with disgust.

"Now what does this girl want?" she asked herself out loud. Vivian contemplated not answering the door - pretending as if she wasn't home - but when she saw the plate of food, she changed her mind and opened the door, but only after Ke-Ke rang the doorbell five times.

"You know, I'm old and slow, but I'm not *deaf.* Don't be ringin' my bell like that; you gon' break it!" fussed Vivian in the usual angry tone that she used to address Ke-Ke.

"I'm so sorry, Grandma Vivian," Ke-Ke sarcastically replied as she stepped into the house. *Smells like old folks and moth balls up in here*, she thought.

"My momma wanted me to bring you this plate of food, since you hadn't been feelin' well lately. Where do you want me to put it?" she asked.

"And just where do you think you should put it? In the kitchen!" Vivian said and then mumbled under her breath as she walked toward the couch.

"What did you say, Grandma?" Ke-Ke asked in a confrontational tone as she turned to face her grandmother. She was tired of her grandmother's evil insults. She was tired of the way her grandmother had mistreated her for as long as she could remember. Ke-Ke knew that she was being disrespectful, but she had been disrespected by her grandmother all of her life and decided that she wasn't going to take it another minute.

"And just *who* do you think you're talkin' to?" asked

Vivian, taken back by Ke-Ke forwardness and attitude.

Ke-Ke took a deep breath while she debated how she would answer and whether or not she was really ready to deal with the can of worms that she had just opened. She saw Vivian seated on the couch, staring up at her with eyes full of fire. That look ended her inner debate; she figured it was time to get to the bottom of the old woman's problem.

"Grandma, I'm talkin' to *you*! You know, for as long as I can remember, you've treated me badly. You never had one nice thing to say to me or about me. You made ugly and evil comments about my appearance, about my daddy; nothin' I ever did was good enough to please you. And believe me, I tried hard to please you for years, until I realized that no matter what I did, you would never treat me like you treat your other grandchildren.

"You wanna know somethin' else? I didn't ask to be here on this earth! So what, you didn't like my daddy? What difference does that make? Seems to me that you got a problem with my skin color, too. Well, guess what? I didn't pick it any more than I asked to be born! You've been an adult all my life, but you've acted like such a spoiled evil kid, poutin' and makin' other people's lives miserable 'cause *you* didn't get your way.

"Haven't you noticed that all of your other grandchildren that you love *so* much are nowhere around? Where are they when you need things? Are they here now bringin' you food?" Ke-Ke was breathing heavily and fighting back her tears as years of anger and frustration came rolling off her tongue. She loved her grandmother very much, but she felt it was time that someone put her in her place, and she was more than happy to do it.

Vivian looked up at Ke-Ke with pure hatred in her eyes, and Ke-Ke could tell that her grandmother was ready to do battle. Right when she opened her mouth to speak, Vivian froze. The fire in her eyes turned cold and she slowly slumped over, hitting her head on the arm of the couch.

"Grandma! Grandma Vivian! Oh, no. Oh, my God!" Ke-Ke ran for the phone to call 911. *I've killed her!* she thought as she told the emergency operator what had just happened. After she hung up with the operator, she called her mother with the news and asked her to meet them at the hospital. Ke-Ke was too ashamed and shaken up to tell her mother all of the details that had preceded her grandmother's collapse. She felt guilty and believed that, whatever had happened to her grandmother, was all her fault.

I
Ke-Ke

The doctors told Cheyenne and Ke-Ke that Vivian had had a stroke. She was completely paralyzed on the left side of her body and would never regain the use of that side, nor would she ever be capable of taking care of herself again. The doctors said that she could still talk a little, but her speech would be jumbled and hard to understand. They suggested that the family make a decision as to whether they would like an in-home nurse to care for Vivian or if they would put her into a nursing home.

While the doctors were talking, Cheyenne cried on her daughter's shoulder as Ke-Ke listened with a face of stone. She couldn't believe what was happening. Many nights as a child she had wished evil things on her grandmother - who she thought of as an evil witch - but never did she think anything would ever happen to her. Ke-Ke always figured that her grandmother had come from the depths of Hell; she was too mean and evil to fall victim to any illness. But now, as she stood in the middle of the cold hospital waiting room, knowing that her Grandma Vivian was down the hall in bed hooked up to tubes, and as she listened to the doctors give their complete diagnosis, she knew that she had been wrong. She realized that in spite of everything, Grandma Vivian was human.

Ke-Ke felt bad for all of the things she had said to her grandmother prior to the stroke, even though it was the truth. She knew that she had to stay strong for her mother, so she pushed back her own feelings of guilt.

Cheyenne had called her brothers and sisters with the news and asked them to come to the hospital. When they arrived, Cheyenne held a family meeting to decide what they would do with their mother and who would be responsible for taking care of her. Ke-Ke sat back in the corner of the room as the siblings argued, fussed, and fought over who wasn't able to do what. Each sibling had an excuse. No one had enough room, enough time, enough money or patience to take care of the woman who had birthed them.

As the argument heated up, Ke-Ke felt it all boiled down to the fact no one had enough *love* to take care of the old woman in her time of need. She didn't speak up either, though, because she really didn't want the responsibility. *Why should I?* she thought, *she never liked me no way.*

The security guard had threatened the group that if they didn't quiet down, they would have to leave. Everyone left the hospital with no decision made, and the burden was left on Cheyenne's shoulders. Cheyenne reluctantly decided a nursing home would be the best option. Ke-Ke and Cheyenne both wondered what Grandma Vivian would think about the decision.

L
Vivian

They've left me here to die in a stinkin' old folks home. I can't believe this! Vivian thought. *I can barely talk, can't do nothin' for myself, and my family done left me here. After all I've done and sacrificed for them, this is how they repay me, by throwin' me in a nursin' home, discardin' me like some ol' trash! Don't none of 'em come visit me 'cause don't none of 'em care.*

Most of these stupid nurses don't like me, neither. They get rough with me sometimes 'cause they know I can't fight back and don't nobody care about me; think they can just do whatever they want...

Her inner conversation was interrupted when Nurse Janna

entered her room.

"Hey, Ms. Vivian. How are you feeling today?" she asked with a smile. "You got your first visitor in eight months. Guess today is your lucky day!"

Janna was the only nurse who was nice to Vivian, and Vivian had grown to like her.

"Yep, Ms. Vivian, there's some pretty young girl here to see you," Nurse Janna said as she escorted Ke-Ke into the room.

"I know I'm the *last* person you want to see, huh?" Ke-Ke asked as she walked into the room behind the nurse.

Vivian's eyes filled with surprise, then anger. She tried to frown at Ke-Ke but the frown was grossly distorted because she couldn't control the left side of her face.

"Nurse, can you please leave us alone for a minute?" Ke-Ke asked.

"Sure, no problem. Just use the buzzer on the right side of the bed if you need anything," Nurse Janna said as she left the room.

Ke-Ke walked around the bed and pulled up a chair. She grabbed Vivian's left hand so that she couldn't pull away.

"First off, I want to say sorry for takin' so long to come and see you. I would say that school kept me away, but the truth is that I felt guilty, guilty for all of the things I said to you. I've been feelin' like I caused your stroke. So, I came to say I'm sorry, sorry for what I said. I was wrong to disrespect you; you're my grandmother and I love you. Since nobody else in the family is willin', I'm gon' take care of you.

"Now, I don't have a house to put you in, but as long as you're here, I'll come and visit you to make sure that you're okay. Hmph, looks like nobody's been in your head for a while…"

Ke-Ke stood up, opened her oversized bag and began unloading hair products, placing them on the nightstand next to the bed. She took the comb and started to untangle her grandmother's long curly hair. Vivian grunted and groaned furiously but Ke-Ke continued on, ignoring the protests. She then pulled out a brush and began brushing Vivian's hair. After a few strokes, Vivian decided to stop fighting and allowed Ke-Ke to make her look beautiful.

Y

Ke-Ke

For six months, Ke-Ke made regular weekly visits to the nursing home to care for her Grandma Vivian, and during that time, a silent bond had formed between them. Ke-Ke showed up like clockwork every Sunday afternoon after church services with new beauty products to lift her grandmother's spirits. Vivian appeared to appreciate the visits and the attention. She became less hostile and resistant toward Ke-Ke; much nicer than she had been during the first few visits. Ke-Ke felt that she and her grandmother were making progress and it made her feel good.

One Sunday afternoon, Ke-Ke arrived at Vivian's room, and noticed that the bed was unmade and there was no one in the room. She turned and saw Nurse Janna coming toward her with a sad look on her face; her stomach started to churn as she anticipated bad news.

"Ke-Ke, I hate to be the bearer of sad news but Vivian passed away a few hours ago. We've been trying to reach your family, but haven't been able to contact anyone yet," Nurse Janna told her.

"She wanted me to give you this when she passed…" the nurse handed Ke-Ke a sealed envelope.

Ke-Ke walked over to the bed and sat down - still reeling from the news of her grandmother's passing - and stared at the sealed envelope.

"She dictated it to me a few months ago," Nurse Janna said. "It was pretty difficult to understand what she was saying and it took us a while to get it right. But we finished it because she was determined and wanted you to have it."

Ke-Ke slowly opened the envelope, pulled out the yellow piece of lined paper and read the letter.

Dear Ke-Ke,
I know I haven't been good to you. I know I
didn't treat you right. And the things that you said
to me, the day I had my stroke, you were right. I
want to say I'm sorry. Thank you for visitin' and
takin' care of me. Thank you for bein' the bigger
person.
I love you.

Grandma Vivian

Ke-Ke folded the letter as tears flowed from her eyes. All of her life she had waited to hear those three words, "I love you" from her grandmother and now she was gone. Ke-Ke knew that her grandmother loved her; she had begun to see the love in her grandmother's eyes every Sunday afternoon when she walked through the door with some new surprise just for her. Ke-Ke tried to console herself with the memories of the good times they had shared during the visits, wishing and willing those memories to erase all of the bad memories from her childhood. She decided that she could and would allow those last memories to be the only memories she had and would pass on about Grandma Vivian. Because now, Ke-Ke felt that they were "family", finally a family.

♀ FOR ONCE IN MY LIFE ♀

For once in my life, I have someone who needs me
Someone I needed so long
For once unafraid, I can go where life leads me
Somehow I know I'll be strong...
For once in my life, I won't let sorrow hurt me
Not like it's hurt me before
For once I have something I know won't desert me
I'm not alone anymore.
For once I can say: This is mine you can't take it
Long as I know I have love I can make it
For once in my life, I have someone who needs me...

(For Once in My Life)

Yolanda rocked back and forth in the oversized rocking chair as she listened to the "oldies but goodies" station on the radio. *I know Stevie never knew that those words would mean what they mean to me*, she thought as she tightened Granny Gee's homemade quilt around her shoulders. Just hearing that song – even though many years had passed – made Yolanda remember the lonely and brokenhearted young girl that she had once been. Hearing that song had always put her in a melancholy mood. So much had happened so fast during that time in her life.

As she rocked slowly, watching the orange and blue flames devour the logs in the fireplace, she tried to pinpoint exactly what had caused her to become a mother at the age of sixteen. Many people figured it was because she was a Black girl

40

living in a low-income neighborhood. Others concluded that she was just "fast" and went wild. Yolanda smirked and shook her head as she considered such ignorant thoughts. Not having much money had nothing to do with her decision to experiment with sex. She had plenty of home training from Granny Gee, and they went to church regularly. She knew all about what God had to say about sex before marriage. Matter of fact, all of those who knew her thought that "Yo-Yo" was a quiet and good girl.

Her decision to give away her virginity also had nothing to do with the fact that her mother had died during her birth due to diabetic complications, and her father had dumped her off on his mother to raise while he worked hard to make a living…and a life for himself.

How much can you be affected by not having a mother that you never knew? Yolanda thought. Her daddy had still been an important part of her life, even though he wasn't around much.

As she continued to rock, the answer managed to slip from behind the mental door where she kept it held hostage.

It all started when Daddy died. That's when all of the pain started, her inner voice whispered.

Yolanda nodded her head in agreement as she swallowed the lump that rose in her throat at the painful admission.

On that cold winter night, as the snow fell quietly to the earth, Yolanda felt inspired to tell her story. She wanted to let the world know that, even though she was labeled as a statistic and a by-product of societal ills by many researchers of the day, she had a story. A story that was filled with pain and confusion, one that could never be measured by surveys, nor would it ever fit neatly into a box of preconceived notions about an ethnic or socio-economic group.

She felt encouraged to tell the world that Yolanda Galient didn't fit the "norm" that supposedly characterized all minority teenage mothers. She smiled a close-lipped half-smile as she reached for her journal and began to write down her innermost thoughts.

I always knew that one day, Daddy would eventually die. Not that he suffered from any major health problems that I knew of – I've just always been a morbid person with a vivid imagination. Guess it comes from being born into death. That's how I think of my life, because my birth killed my mother. I remember once when I was ten years old, I told my older cousin, Eric, that my Daddy "must be dead" because he hadn't called me in such a long time. I was really nonchalant when I said it, mainly because I was angry with Daddy for neglecting me and leaving me with Granny Gee. I didn't understand why I couldn't live with him. I was just being ugly acting that day and talking out of my hurt feelings. I don't think Eric liked my statement or my attitude, because he made me call Daddy's house and talk to him. I felt so much better after I talked to Daddy. I was so glad that my Daddy was in my life and that he was alive. I loved him so much.

I must say the reality of Daddy dying on me was much more than I ever thought of or imagined during any one of my many morbid moments. I remember the night the call came. I was and am to this day weary of late-night calls. It always seems the person on the other end is calling with some information that you really don't want to hear. I was sleeping good and hard when the ringing of the phone woke me up. I really wasn't trying to listen to the conversation— any other time I would have just gone back to sleep – but something was keeping me awake, and

*I could hear bits and pieces of what was being
said. I remember hearing Granny Gee's voice and
her change of tone; I immediately knew that
something was definitely wrong. After listening a
bit longer, I knew that someone had died and it
was a man. My first thought was that my cousin
Sandy had lost her husband, and I started to feel
sorry for his little girl, who was close to my age.
They hadn't been at the family reunion because he
was ill. He had had a heart attack a couple of
days before, and I assumed he just didn't make it.
Right when I was about to say a prayer for my
little cousin, Granny Gee asked a question that
pierced my heart and held my attention. She asked
the caller, "Do they suspect foul play?"*

*Foul play? It couldn't have been my cousin
who died if she was asking about foul play. That
one question told my soul something that my
conscious mind didn't want to acknowledge at the
time, and it caused me to get up. I remember
getting out of my bed and walking toward the
light coming from Granny Gee's room.*

*I don't know how long it took me to walk to
her room; everything seemed to go in slow
motion. When I got to her doorway and looked at
her, she told the caller, "Oh no, she heard me!"*

*In all honesty, I never heard her mention
Daddy or that anything had happened to him, but
when I looked at her, I knew– my soul knew – who
had died, and I heard someone screaming "No!"
over and over again. The screams were loud and
sorrowful; I didn't even know that I was the one
screaming until I was facedown at the foot of
Granny Gee's bed and her covers muffled my
cries. The only thing I knew at that point was that*

he was gone; Daddy had left me. The man whom I loved most in the whole world had deserted me.

I was his "Baby Girl" – the term he lovingly called me – how could he do this to me? He had left me with a hole in my heart and in my world, and there was no one to fill it.

Granny Gee stayed calm throughout the rest of the conversation. I found out that she was talking to Uncle Eli when she asked for the details of Daddy's death. Daddy had had a heart attack and died alone in his apartment. Alone. He had been dead for three days when his landlord discovered his body.

Three days? I was angry with Daddy for staying so distant. If he had kept in touch with the family more often, there would have been no way he could have been left there, dead, for three days. I secretly hated myself for not being able to live with him. If I had been there, then maybe he could have been saved. I could have helped somehow.

As I beat myself up in the midst of my grief, I remember Granny Gee telling Uncle Eli to make all of the funeral arrangements. A funeral? Daddy's funeral? It wasn't real to me; none of this is happening, I thought to myself. But the funeral did indeed take place.

Before the funeral started, I went into the small viewing room with the coffin to see Daddy and talk to him. I tapped my fingers lightly on the lid of the coffin as I tried to think of something to say. The cold coffin resounded under my touch; it made the sound of one lightly tapping on a hollow pipe with a penny. I touched it in hopes of making it seem real to my heart and mind– to try to make sense out of what was happening–but I couldn't.

They had him in a gold-toned coffin, and there were instructions that it was to stay closed at all times. There were a couple of different versions of the reason why it couldn't be opened for viewing. I was told that the body had badly decomposed while it was in his apartment for those three hot days; another reason I was given as to why the casket couldn't be opened was that all ten children needed to be present, and that couldn't happen because no one knew how to contact my other paternal siblings. Why did Daddy have to be a "rolling stone?"

I was angry because I needed to see him. I didn't believe that my Daddy –who was a good six feet, four inches –was in a coffin that looked like my five-foot, six-inch frame could barely fit in it. I refused to believe that he had left me. He wouldn't just leave me, because he loved me too much. But in spite of my desire to see him, the funeral was closed casket.

The funeral home had small lights in the ceiling. It looked like a starry night sky when the lights were dimmed; I thought it was a classy touch. Overall, it was a quiet service. There were no loud outbursts, fainting, or other typical funeral theatrics. I refused to cry, and didn't shed one tear during the entire service. I just sat there on the second pew between my Auntie Dorothy and my cousin Eric, and listened to what was being said, all the while staring at the poster-sized picture of my Daddy.

It was cropped from a picture that had been taken of me and Daddy at my sixth birthday party. Standing next to him, I looked like Daddy had "spit me out on the ground," as the old folks would say. We had the same golden brown skin tone, the same almond eyes and the same high foreheads on our long slim faces. Looking at that picture next to the coffin made me feel close to him.

    In the middle of the service, I rushed out to go to the restroom. Granny Gee came straight after me; I think she must've thought that I was upset and couldn't take being in there any longer. When she met up with me in the restroom, I let her know that I was fine and just had to "use it." I'm sure that my lack of emotion probably unnerved her, but I was dealing with it all the best way that I could. I had convinced myself that Daddy wasn't dead. He had left me and gone somewhere, but he wasn't dead.
    When I went back into the service, there was a somewhat awkward moment going on. A family friend who was on the program couldn't figure out how to get to the podium and my Auntie Barbara was whispering the directions to him. I guess the guy couldn't hear her, because she eventually had to raise her voice to instruct him on which way to go. I thought it was pretty funny, so I started laughing out loud. Everyone looked at me, thinking that I had finally "broke down." They were shocked to see that I was laughing. That was the moment that I learned how to laugh to keep from crying.
    When it came time to "view" the casket and picture, I refused to go up with the procession. I could see quite well from where I was sitting and, –having it in my mind that my Daddy wasn't in

that coffin, – I felt no need to pretend.

Afterward, there was a short service at the gravesite. Daddy had requested to be buried in the same grave as his father, Pappy Gee. I grabbed a few flowers from the top of the coffin and was then ready to leave. I felt that there was no need to stay around while some stranger got buried.

For days before the funeral and for months afterward, I would call Daddy's home number and let it ring, hoping with all of my being that he would pick up and tell me how much he loved me. I continued to call the number even after it had been disconnected. One day, my heart skipped a beat when I dialed the number, it rang, and someone finally answered.

Unfortunately, it wasn't Daddy. Someone who worked for a beauty salon answered; the number had been reassigned. I got angry with the phone company for taking Daddy's phone number and giving it to someone else. I knew in my heart that he would need it again one day.

Around my house, life went on. Before Daddy's "death," Granny Gee had been in the process of getting custody of my cousin Cheryl's little twin boys, because Cheryl was strung out on that "stuff" and the babies were born addicted to drugs. The process finalized shortly after the funeral, and now there were two new needy additions to the household. I was less than thrilled, all the while still grieving.

Depression and suicidal thoughts had taken up permanent residence in my heart and mind. I laughed a lot to try to keep from crying, but I cried much more than I laughed. I isolated myself and felt as if I no longer had anyone in the world who loved me. I had recently broken up with my boyfriend, Granny Gee's attention was focused on the new babies, and Daddy had left me. I felt alone, invisible, like I had been abandoned in the world. I just wanted to die; I wanted all of the pain to end. But suicide was not the route that I chose to take to ease my pain.

That following spring, my boyfriend Donte and I decided to try to work things out between us. We had broken up because he told me that he had slept with a girl and gotten her pregnant, but she didn't keep the baby. He had been trying to get me to sleep with him, but I was determined that I was saving my virginity for marriage; he just had to deal with it or leave me alone. After he confessed to cheating on me, I ended the relationship, but time had healed some of those wounds, so I was willing to give us another chance.

One afternoon, Donte' walked me home from school and we discussed some of the issues in our past. I had some questions that I wanted answered about what had really happened between us. From that conversation, I learned that Donte' had lied to me, made up the entire story about the mystery girl, just to make me jealous because I wouldn't sleep with him. I stayed calm on the outside, but on the inside I was boiling over with anger. How could he lie to me like that and cause me so much pain and humiliation? After everything else that I had gone through and was going through at that time -oh, I knew he would have to pay for the pain that he had caused me! I knew better than to be vengeful, but I was determined to hurt him the same way that he had hurt me.

I led him to believe that we were going to work out our differences, even though I had decided to find someone else to be with and planned on throwing it in his face. That would teach him...so I thought.

I found the perfect candidate for my revenge plot. He was the total opposite of Donte', inside and out, the two were as different as night and day. Donte' was short, dark-skinned and stocky, while Shiloh was tall, light-skinned and thin. Shiloh was actually the total opposite of me as well, - being he was a straight "A" student and I struggled just to get my homework finished - but I figured that he would do, as long as I could make Donte' pay. Shiloh wasn't the least bit interested in me, but I chased after him anyway and gave Donte' the impression that I was so in love.

I hurt Donte' badly with my plot for revenge, and what was even more unfortunate was that I got caught up in my own deception. It all backfired on me! I ended up actually liking Shiloh and playing out the last piece of my revenge...I gave Shiloh what I told Donte' no man would ever have without marriage -my virginity.

As a result, I became pregnant the first time that I ever had sex. Thinking back, I can still hear that inner voice telling me that if I slept with Shiloh I would get pregnant, but I didn't listen. Truth be told, I didn't even enjoy the encounter! I found it to be quite painful and highly overrated. My friends had really lied to me about the joys of doing "IT."

I found out I was pregnant when my period

didn't make its monthly appearance. I knew I was in big trouble. I didn't know what I would tell Granny Gee or how I would take care of a child; I was only fifteen! The only thing that I knew was that there was a little someone growing inside of me who was mine. All mine. I wanted the baby to be a boy, because with so many male family members, I felt that I understood boys better than girls. I knew that like Daddy - who was not dead, just missing - my little baby would love me just for me.

I fell in love with him from the moment that I knew he existed inside of my body. My love for my baby filled the hole left in my heart and my world that was created when Daddy left me. With my baby on the way, I felt that I didn't need Donte or Shiloh anymore!

Reality came crashing into my world quickly. Granny Gee hit the ceiling when she found out that I was expecting. With Cheryl's twins and our limited income - along with the fact that I was only fifteen - it almost gave her a stroke. She told the whole family that I was pregnant, and they all had an opinion. I received many phone calls from well-meaning family members with something "helpful" to say.

The only person that I wanted to hear from was Daddy. I secretly hoped that someone in the family who knew that he wasn't dead - someone who knew where he really was - would tell him what his "Baby Girl" had done. I figured that if he knew what I had done, he would come back to me.

It wasn't a big shock to me to realize that no one in my family wanted me to have the baby. As

*frightened and unsure as I was about my future -
and about the baby on the way - I knew I couldn't
and wouldn't kill him. I felt that I needed him as
much as I needed air to breathe. My baby was the
key to my world, the someone who would love me.
There was no way I was giving him up for anyone!*

*Shiloh didn't want the baby either and was no
help during my home turmoil. I didn't expect him
to be of much support; he was just a boy who
fathered a child. By the time that I was three
months pregnant, Shiloh had packed his bags and
gone away to the first out of state college that had
accepted him. I wasn't hurt for too long behind
his leaving though; I had my baby.*

*By God's grace, I made it through most of my
sophomore year of high school and had a smooth
and easy pregnancy. The labor part was pretty
rough though, it hurt more than I could ever have
imagined. I was in labor for thirty-six hours! It
was thirty-six hours of horrendous physical
stress; I felt as if I was being taken to the brink of
death with every contraction and, just as quickly,
I was being snatched back, with the full
knowledge that I would have to repeat the
experience within the next few minutes! It was an
experience that I hadn't counted on, but after it
was all over, I was finally able to lay my eyes on
my little bundle of love, my baby boy, Jonathan.*

*With the birth of my beautiful baby boy, I
figured that I once again had someone in this
world who would love me. He saw the beauty in
me and didn't want to leave me. He was someone
who would love me just because I loved him. And
he needed me; no one on this earth was more
important to him than I was. I could finally tell*

*the whole world, "This love is mine and you can't
take it!" I felt I could truly say, for once in my life
I have love and it's for real.*

*Now, years later, as I have grown into a
woman, I know that what I was looking for at that
time only comes from God. I didn't know it at the
time, but I was really looking for someone to
depend on, not a dependent. As I have learned to
look to and depend on God, I realize that having a
child - while I was so young and unmarried -
wasn't the best choice or His choice for my life
but He has blessed me in spite of my
shortcomings. Single parenting, I will admit, has
been tough and much more than I bargained for
but I wouldn't trade my wonderful little boy for
the world. I can say this, I now know that, for
once in my life I do have a true and unconditional
love, the love that I had been searching and
longing for ... and it comes from God.*

Yolanda grabbed the box of Kleenex from the table and
wiped the tears that were streaming down her face. The room
around her was much cooler; the fire had burned completely out,
leaving only glowing orange coals in the dark fireplace. The clock
on the wall read 3:52 a.m., definitely much later than she planned
on staying up. Yolanda got up out of the rocking chair and placed
her journal next to the computer. She planned to type up her entry
later that morning.

"It'll be the first chapter of my book for teenage girls,"
she said to herself. After she readied herself for bed, she walked
down the hall and looked into the bedroom where her son slept
soundly. Yolanda couldn't help but smile as she watched him
sleep. She noted that beside the fact he had a lighter skin tone than
she did, Jonathan was her male "twin." She bent down, kissed him

on his forehead and got into his bed with him. As remnants of the song from the radio floated in her head, Yolanda softly hummed the rest of the tune, as she drifted off to sleep.

♀   ♀

<u>PART II</u>

<u>~BEING GROWN</u>

"Being grown" is DEFINITELY
Not what I had expected it to be!
Lord, have mercy,
Mercy on me!

♀   ♀

I'M PERFECTLY NORMAL

I wonder, why do I allow caring for somebody to turn into an obsession? Does it come from my habitual tendency to live in the past, or are the men I meet really too good to let go of? I don't think so! I can't recall one single instance, deed, or dating experience that convinced me any particular partner was a vital organ and his removal would mean sudden death. You wouldn't know it by my actions, though! It has to come from my tendency to live in the past and my resistance to change. Anybody can agree there's nothing great about having a man in your life who lies to you, and eventually, breaks your heart. I seem to thrive on that type of drama. I guess most women do. We love men so much and are too busy looking at the "potential being"; we ignore the imperfect beings that we interact with daily. Don't get me wrong; all men aren't bad. They just all have faults. I hope one day I'll learn to love a man for his faults instead of loving him in spite of his faults. You know, fully accepting him "as-is." I'm constantly digging in my bag of tricks to miraculously change him into who I want him to be or who I think he should be. The harder he resists, the more persistent and pursuant I become.

It's so weird. The world around us glorifies "being in love." We're shown what it's supposed to be like, but there's no handbook on how to stay that way. Nobody mentions the heartache, or that for every high, there's a low. Personally, I think the idea of "being in love" is highly overrated. I've been there enough to know. The romance, flowers, and the sweet talk only last so long. It's been proven to me that most people believe once all of that ends; the "love" is gone. I haven't met a man yet who knew how to make a relationship work. Were they really just that ignorant or did they have another game plan in mind? The men whom I've dealt with must've had another game plan in mind. Problems came, they split. Have you ever seen a man who loved his woman? It's a beautiful sight. He would walk over fire and swallow glass to keep her happy and safe. His whole world revolves around her. There's nothing that he wouldn't do or go through for her. I'm *quite* sure no man has ever loved me. I'm sure they liked me a whole lot, but of course, that wasn't enough. If it was, I wouldn't be alone now. I know that sounds pathetic, but I've been told that healing comes when a person takes a step back and looks at them self honestly, when they look at the events in their life and see things not as they wanted them to be or how they thought things should have been, but simply as things *were*. I'm looking at things honestly right now, and yes, it's pretty pathetic. Guess I'm healed now, right?

Just out of boredom, I looked up synonyms for the words "love," "caring," and "obsession." The amazing thing to me was that love and caring seem to share meanings such as "devotedly attached," "cherished," "being fond of," and "tenderness." "Obsession" means none of these things. No person I know would ever confuse a tormented conscience with love. There's nothing romantic about being haunted, crazed, and perplexed. The word obsession had a lot more in common with the synonyms for psychopath than with love. The more words I came across, the more uncomfortable I began to feel. Besides the fact that the synonyms described my behavioral and relational patterns, it all sounded so twisted and sick! What disturbed me most was that everybody I know relates to others in this fashion, and it's called love. In fact, the society we live in promotes this type of "love" in the music we listen to, the books we read, and the movies we see. The idea is planted that we can't live without someone, we should never let them go, and that it's perfectly all right to just stop breathing because we don't have them in our lives. I didn't find one word describing love that meant pain, being disrespected, abuse, or death. Yet, we've been taught that love hurts sometimes, and maybe it's not love if it doesn't. Nobody ever came right out and said it; I learned the "love equals pain" equation through example. If this equation made any kind of sense, it would mean that every man in my life truly loved me!

You know what I really hate? When people assume, insinuate, or come right out and say I need a man in my life! It's like they think a man is the remedy to any problem that I have. It amazes me how everybody - including men - has been reared toward thinking that women need men. Don't get me wrong - I'm no bra-burning feminist - but it's harmful to a person's esteem to believe they aren't complete without someone or something. How can you fully love yourself when you don't feel that you're all you're supposed to be? How can you truly be happy with yourself when you believe that who you are depends on whether or not you have a man? It's not fair! I wonder if men feel less "manly" without a woman? Well, some men feel like they need three or four women to truly be a "man," which is just as sick as being an obsessive woman.

I'm talking to you as if we've known each other forever. I still haven't gotten around to introducing myself or explaining why I've decided to talk to you today. What's your name, anyway? Oh, okay, nice to meet you. My name? Well, my name isn't important, because if you can see yourself in anything that I have to say, then I'm just like you. What? Why did I decide to talk to you? Well, because some people can't relate to my feelings; some folks have never felt that they loved somebody so much that they just couldn't let go. I think you can relate, so I guess I'll give you what I like to call the "inside scoop." An invitation into the mind of the obsessed -people, like me, who truly don't believe that others have the right to walk away from a relationship and firmly believe in the motto, "It ain't over until *I* say it is!" I'm sure you're familiar with this. Honestly, we know this mind set doesn't work, but we can't give up until we've exhausted every effort, played every card, and sometimes until we'd rather die than live without that person. No holds barred when you believe that somebody holds something you used to just *want,* but now you *need.* Or when you believe that you have and are what they need. You'll spend all of your money, travel thousands of miles, disregard friends and family, and totally forego your physical, mental, spiritual, and emotional well-being, all for a fixation that isn't anybody else's reality. It's only real in your mind. Hmph, might as well be a crack-head!

I would like to say events in my childhood laid the foundation for this problem of mine. But everybody and their momma has used this lame excuse for everything under the sun that's deemed unacceptable in our culture. Who made up the list of what's acceptable and what's not, anyway? God says a lot of things that make up this "Acceptable/Unacceptable" list, but people – including myself – are so hypocritical. Half the time we're out doing our own thing, not caring what God has said and doing everything contrary to it. The minute something comes up that we can't accept – that's contrary to our personal opinions and beliefs –what God has to say becomes *so* important. Makes you think, huh?

I believe events beget events. Choices, whether we made them or not, choose the flow of the events. Please don't think I'm trying to dismiss the fact that experiences from the past do affect the person that you become; just bear with me a minute. See, from the moment one-half of me met the other half in my mother's womb, my foundation was set. I've come to accept the fact that I had no control then and have limited control now. I've learned that I can only control the way that I deal with situations when they come into my life.

I realize that my first relationship with a man was filled with broken promises and physical distance. That relationship has affected the way that I relate to men to this day. My father wasn't around much while I grew up. My dad would call and promise me things that never came to be. I developed the attitude "He didn't mean to lie to me. When he says he'll make it up to me, he will." Well, he *never* made it up to me. I just kept getting lifted up only to be let down, and I forgave him every time. I thought that if I just believed in him, he would change and start to do the things he said he would. I was definitely a child! Yet I've carried that same child-like notion into my relationships with men. I give fifth and sixth chances to men who didn't even deserve a first chance. In my mind, I believe that they'll finally realize that I'm a good woman worth treating right, if only I'm patient, understanding, and forgiving. Just because they hurt me before doesn't mean that they'll do it again. Yeah, right! As I've grown, I've learned that people will do whatever you let them do to you and they won't change unless you take drastic measures. People won't stop hurting you unless you make them stop.

Let's see…I'm trying to figure out when I crossed that thin line between "I love you so much" to "I'll kill you or myself, if you leave me." I think it was a slow and natural progression, just like every other disease. Starting with my first stress filled, highly dramatic relationship, I gave all I had to try to hold on to somebody who didn't want me in the first place. Take notes here…if you notice that somebody isn't interested in you, there's nothing on this earth you can do that will change their mind. The key word here is "change." I tried everything that I knew to try to change Malik. He just had to love me like I loved him. The more "love" I gave him, the more drama I got in return -confirming the theory that love equals pain – which therefore led me to believe that he loved me. So what if he would treat me like the least important thing in the world, humiliate and disrespect me every time he felt like it? It didn't matter to me because we were "in LOVE." I thought giving myself to him would be the most persuasive tool that I could use to get him where I wanted him. Don't misunderstand me now; I did love him with all of my heart, it's just a rule of human nature - everybody has a motive for what they do. Whether it's an honest or manipulative motive, now that's the real question. Remember this…nobody ever does anything that they won't benefit from, whether the benefit is physical, mental, or emotional.

Anyway, back to what I was saying. Giving myself to him

didn't change things between us. Ha, I can laugh now because I was too stupid to see then what was really going on. I wanted him to validate my self-worth because I didn't believe that I was worth much. I was forcing myself on him so that his love could possibly become the love that I should've had for myself. The more he hurt me, the more confirmation was given to the idea that I was worthless. I was asking him to do for me what I couldn't readily do for myself.

What did I learn from this relationship? Well, because of the heartache, I learned that you should never look to anybody else for what you can do for and should give to yourself. But the lesson cost me a lot emotionally, even physically - I still have the razor scars on my wrist to prove it.

Malik hurt me badly and I wanted him to hurt just as much as I did. Haven't you ever been hurt so badly by somebody that you wanted them to suffer just as much as you had? And if you couldn't make them suffer, your heart still wanted vengeance, crying out that *somebody* had to pay, even if you were the one who suffered by not eating or sleeping, by isolating yourself, or even by trying to take your own life? The Bible constantly reminds us that vengeance is the Lord's. You want to know why? Because it's human nature to want to repay others for the wrong that they've done to us. So, I tried to make Malik pay for hurting me by hurting myself…but it didn't hurt him or bring him back to me.

Changing the subject, I've been thinking and I've realized that when a person loves others in as strongly possessive manner as I do, others in their life have usually loved them that way. As much as I pride myself on being a healthy heterosexual, I've realized that there have been women in my life who have related to me as I have related to men. It was all under the disguise of friendship. It's weird. If a woman relates to you with the same - or sometimes stronger - intensity that most women relate to men, does that make her an undercover lesbian? I really don't know the answer to that one. I do know that, as a woman, there comes a point when you can't trust or really be close to other women.

Everything is okay when you and all of your friends don't have men in your lives, but when a man enters the picture, things definitely change. Have you ever been in a relationship when your friends weren't, and they started to act differently toward you? It's happened to me; I've done it myself and I've witnessed it dozens of times. Misery loves company, and if you're happy, every measure must be taken to get you back into the lonely-hearts club. It's truly sad. But it's just one of the many reasons why I don't fool with females nowadays.

Now, back in the day, when I did believe in female friends, I had two friends that were particularly dear to my heart. I'm trying to figure out which one to tell you about, or if I should even tell you at all. Mmmm, I really don't know you that well yet to tell you all of my business. How about this...I'll let you know about the females at another time and we'll stick with the stories about the men for now...all right?

Okay, where was I? Oh, yeah. It seemed to have come from thin air. All of a sudden from friends, family, and my inner self came this pressure to be married. It's like I just woke up one morning and any man that I was dating was going to be my husband, no matter what he wanted. I had a collection of wedding magazines, invitation catalogs; you name it and I had it. I was just waiting for the day when Mr. Right would come along. Looking back, I can see where my disease went from being a mild illness to a critical condition. Due to the ending of this particular relationship, I suffered an emotional and maybe even mental breakdown.

It makes no earthly sense to be so attached to somebody that you're willing to let yourself wither up and die rather than live without them. Sadly enough, that's exactly what I tried to do. When I met Shawn, I was slowly getting over Malik; I'm a slow emotional healer. I really wasn't looking for a relationship at that time; I was just starting to have fun dating again. I met Shawn at a nightclub and, truthfully, I wasn't interested in him. First off, I had no clue as to what he really looked like, and I definitely didn't want a "strobe-light honey." You know, the ones who look good in the dark but *horrible* in the light. I wasn't trying to ruin my image by dating an ugly guy.

Shawn asked for my phone number without pen or paper. He said he would memorize it. I didn't expect him to remember my number or to call me. Ha, I really didn't care if he called or not. It's so strange, it seems that the men I've met whom I wasn't really interested in at all in the beginning ended up breaking my heart the worst. I'll admit nobody ever had or will break my heart like Shawn did.

Shawn worked hard to win me over, and eventually, I let down my guard and started to care about him. That's when everything changed. All of a sudden, I found myself pursuing him! We went out less and less. I called him and received fewer and fewer return phone calls. Quality time became a thing of the past. The more distant he became, the more needy and persistent I became. I wanted to marry him. I wanted to have his children; I knew that I could be the best wife he'd ever dreamed of. I had our life perfectly pictured in my head. It was reality to me; I was just waiting for it to manifest into his reality. But it never did.

I hung in there, though, trying desperately to fulfill a dream, my dream. I ignored every sign, banner, billboard, and public service announcement that the relationship just wasn't right. I wanted it to be right, so I made it right…in my mind. Shawn finally broke up with me after seven months of dragging the dead relationship around. Truthfully, the relationship was over after three months, but I held on until he called it quits.

When it ended, I was crushed. I experienced a severe bout of depression and starved myself. I lost over sixty pounds. Being I only weighed one hundred and forty pounds to begin with, I was hospitalized and force-fed intravenously until I decided to eat again. I was *sure* that when Shawn found out that I was in the hospital he'd come back to me, especially after seeing what his leaving had done. But he didn't come by the hospital to see me and he didn't come back to me.

Looking back, I believe that I was hurt more because I wasn't getting married; losing him was just a technicality. Again I didn't get what I wanted, again I got hurt, so once again I hurt myself.

Off the subject, I just thought of something! I believe that everything is revealed to you only when you're ready, and this just popped into my head. As I think back over all of this, I realize the only way that I'll ever get over my issues is to remember the good times and move on. And if there weren't many good times, I'll have to forgive the other person - and myself - and simply get over it. The world keeps turning every second, no matter what; life still goes on around me. I can't allow my world or my life to stop because of a man. A man didn't make me and I shouldn't let one break me.

You know what? I don't need a man! Whether I'm single or married, I'm complete just as I am. I've grown to know that it's not the men that I've been obsessed with, it's being in love. The possibilities of it all and the challenges to keep that good feeling - that's what I'm addicted to. I just have to learn how to cope when the good feelings leave. I've heard it said that letting go is the greatest balm for the wounded heart. I've really been working on it, you know, letting go. All of these daily sessions have been paying off...

Oh no, here they come! Ugh, I didn't know what time it was; time has flown by so quickly! Thanks for stopping by and listening to me. I really like visits. Nobody comes to see me, nor does anybody ever *really* listen to me around here; they just keep trying to "fix" me.

Well, I need to take my three o'clock medication and the hospital has very strict guidelines for those of us who reside in the "J" ward here in the state mental institution. "No visitors close to medication time," that's what they always say. They think the last dose may have worn off or something. As soon as you leave, they'll release me from this uncomfortable straightjacket. I'd really like to stretch my arms out a bit.

I don't know why the doctors think it's necessary to give me this medication or to keep me in this straightjacket; I overheard a nurse say that I need to be kept "calm and sane." They think that I'm dangerous and that I might hurt myself again…or that I might hurt somebody else. But, I'm not insane; I'm perfectly normal! I get angry, jealous, vengeful, hurt, I love, I cry, I laugh. As you can tell, I do know what's right and what's wrong. *Okay*, I do acknowledge that I've been working through some issues, but one of the nurses gave me a really nice Bible to read a few months ago and it's helped me a lot to know that, even if I never receive the love of a man, God loves me. I am even learning what love truly is -and it doesn't equal pain. Yep, I'll be out of here one day, hey, maybe I'll come and visit *you*. Don't look so worried, when I'm released, you can rest assured; I'll be just fine.

PEOPLE IN MY BUSINESS

"Girl, why you guys still ain't engaged?? What's takin' him so long? It's been over a year; what else does he need to know about you before he decides that he wants to be married to you?"

Richelle pulled the receiver from her ear and tried to find a focal point to concentrate on as her niece, Mickey, ranted and raved about the pace of Richelle and Raymond's relationship. Richelle wondered to herself how someone as petite as Mickey could have such a big mouth.

*One, two, three, four...*Richelle began taking a mental count of the leaves on her ivy. As the centerpiece for her living room table, it was a beautiful addition, and gave her condo a comfortable feel -so she thought. Mickey was still on the other end of the phone - high up on her soapbox - giving her unwanted opinion about her younger aunt's relationship.

Somebody needs to give Mickey a clue, Richelle thought. *Bein' older don't always mean bein' wiser, and personally she's gettin' on my last nerve. Shoot, if I had a dollar for all of the bad advice she's given me over the years, I'd be* paid*! It's time to end this conversation!*

"Uh, Mickey, girl, I forgot that I gotta go pick up some stuff from the store before Ray gets here. Let me call you back." Richelle knew that this probably wasn't going to shut her niece up - let alone get her off the phone - but she figured that it was worth a try.

"Oh no, you don't, Shelly!!" Mickey's voice rose an octave as she continued on her warpath of know-it-all-ness.

"I know you, and you're *always* organized and prepared for everything. You don't have to go nowhere. You just don't want to hear what I have to say. Well, you know what, Shelly?

The truth hurts sometimes, and if you keep wastin' your time with Ray, you'll never find Mr. Right.

"Have some faith in God. God don't want us to suffer, nor does He make things so frustratin' or hard. You know what I say...if it's too hard, it must not be meant. If he ain't makin' a move to marry you, then you need to find somebody else. You ain't gettin' no younger!"

Richelle rolled her eyes, sighed, and thought, *Mickey* must *be on her period or somethin' because she's determined to annoy me today!*

"Look, Mickey, I love you, but I gotta go. I'll call you later." *Lord forgive me for lyin',* Richelle prayed. She knew that she wasn't going to call Mickey anytime later that day, and she probably wouldn't even call her later on in the week.

"Hmph. All right then, be that way. *Bye!!*" Mickey sounded very agitated, but Richelle didn't care. She just placed the phone back on the base and shook her head.

"I definitely didn't need that phone call, especially not today," Richelle said as she went over to the refrigerator and pulled out some grapes. "Nervous eating. I need to quit doin' this unless I want to gain even more weight! I'm short and chubby as-is. This extra thirty-five pounds that I've gained is not beggin' for company. Now, that would not be cute!" She looked around and laughed out loud. "I know I'm goin' crazy, because I'm talkin' to myself. Look what well-meanin' family can do to a sista!"

Richelle began to think about how she and Raymond had been arguing for the past few days over the status of their relationship and the direction that it was going.

"I really hate that we're both on opposite sides and compromise seems to be nowhere in sight," she said to herself. Richelle popped a grape in her mouth as she stared at the wall and tried to calm her nerves.

"To make matters worse," she continued as she picked over the grapes, "every female in my immediate family is ready and waitin' to plan my wedding, and they are puttin' major pressure on me to give them a date. Whenever I let them know that me and Ray aren't even engaged yet, the lectures, the questions, all of the unwanted advice on how to 'handle' him, and, eventually, the nasty arguments start.

"It doesn't matter where we are either; it could be the weekly Sunday dinners, the monthly girls' shopping trip, or even the church parking lot. When somebody brings up me and Ray, the mess hits the fan."

Richelle grabbed a handful of grapes and walked into her bedroom, all the while talking to herself.

"I remember this one time, a nice elderly sister of the congregation made the mistake of askin' about Ray within earshot of Momma and Mickey. I'm surprised we didn't get banned from the congregation for all the ruckus that we caused!" Richelle said as she giggled, remembering the commotion.

"Momma even had the *nerve* to try to bring the preacher into the argument, askin' for scriptures on marriage and tryin' to make him say that it was sinful for a man to keep a woman waitin' for marriage longer than six months. It was simply amazin' how she tried to make the scriptures fit my relationship!" Richelle sighed as she reminisced and thought more about her family.

"It never fails; whenever and wherever me and Ray are mentioned, there will be a long drawn out discussion about why we aren't engaged yet, let alone married. Most of the women in my family make me feel like an outcast because they're all married. They blame me for bein' patient – also known as bein' soft with no backbone, as they so lovingly put it - and curse Ray for bein' a 'good for nothin' no-count Negro.' Even Grandma Hannah will put in her teeth to jump into the conversation and give her two cents about my 'situation.'

"Lord, help me!" Richelle said as she threw herself backward on her bed, fighting back the tears that were welling up in her eyes. She thought about calling her best friend Mariah and crying in her ear for the next half hour, but decided against it. "I'm pretty sure *everybody* is tired of me whinin' about this relationship!" she said to the ceiling. Over and over in her head, Richelle kept hearing all of the advice from her family and friends.

You have to decide when you've had enough. Pray to God to find out if he's even the one. You might not want to hear this, but he may not be the one. The phrase that Richelle hated to hear the most was, *"Girl, just leave him alone. You're better off without him!"*

Richelle propped her hands behind her head and listened to the beautiful watch that Ray had given her for her birthday tick-tock in her ear.

It sounds like a tickin' time bomb, she thought, *ready to explode at any moment if Ray doesn't burst through the door and propose marriage to me. And if he does come through the door and propose, he has to have a platinum and diamond engagement ring to properly defuse the bomb.* Richelle giggled at her silly thoughts as she wiped away a runaway tear before it got into her ear.

"Yeah, there's a 'bomb' all right," she said, "and it's called my family. But that's what happens when you allow too many people into your relationship. They feel that they have the right to comment on anything and everything after you run to them with a problem, or two, or three," Richelle rationalized. "I'll admit that I've been way too open about our relationship and my frustrations.

"Man, do I ever regret that mistake!" Richelle groaned as she continued her one-way conversation with her ceiling. "If this thing with me and Ray doesn't work out, the next relationship that I'm in will be so private. I might not even let anyone know that I'm seein' someone until after I've eloped!"

Richelle shifted her body so that her head was hanging slightly over the side of the bed and started to talk to a crack in the wall near the doorframe.

"It's bad enough that Ray and I can't get on the same page, but to have all of this outside pressure, well, it's too much for me right now. Don't they understand that I do *want* to get married, but I can't force anybody to do anything? A marriage - the last time I checked - consisted of a man and a woman who *both* wanted to get married, of their own free will and at the same time.

"I've dated this man for over a year. Yes, some do consider a year enough time to at least know if you'd be interested in spendin' your life with someone. I'd say that's a valid statement. But Ray and I have a long distance relationship, and things just don't work out for us the way that things work in those relationships where the people stay in the same town. We have had to get really creative about everything just to make it this far!

"We've been especially creative about our methods of communication, 'cause Lord knows I can't get my phone cut off again. May God bless the creator of email and instant messenger; those things have truly saved this relationship! We have so many other obstacles to face, not includin' the normal issues that come with a man and woman being together!"

Richelle turned over onto her stomach and continued to plead her case to the small dark-brown teddy bear that Ray had won for her at a carnival last summer.

"I'm tryin' to be patient with him and with myself, you know? Overall - outside of the distance and the pace of things - I think Ray and I have a good thing goin' here. He ain't cheatin' on me, and I *know* that the man truly loves me. He's the best man I've ever dated in my life and he treats me with respect. Now how often do you find that?

"I'm now wise enough to finally want and appreciate a good man and Ray's a good man –not perfect but good. We have a lot in common, too. We have our love for Christ, we have similar hobbies and interests, and we really enjoy each other as friends and as significant others. We complement each other in the areas where we haven't already completed each other. My family doesn't want to hear that, though. They just want to see a ring on my finger and a white dress on my body, preferably yesterday."

Richelle changed positions and tried to get comfortable, to no avail. She stacked a few pillows behind her back to create a cushion between her body and the wall so that she could sit up. She then picked up the teddy bear and placed it in her cross-legged lap so that she could have its undivided attention.

"I've rushed into so many past relationships only to rush out of them with my feelings hurt and pieces of my soul missin', never to be recovered. I just want it to be right this time. I've always wanted a man who knew how to make a relationship work. I just didn't know that it would take so much time or energy. Guess it's true that you have to be careful what you pray for, huh?

"What? What did you say? No, I'm not makin' excuses for him! Yes, I do think that I should at least have a promise ring by now, somethin' outside of his word that assures me of where we're headed. I've been nothin' but good to him and patient with him. I was there for him when he was laid off, helpin' him out when he needed it.

"Huh? Yeah, sometimes it burdened me, but I survived. Love can make you do some crazy things, givin' when you don't have and sacrificin' when you know you shouldn't. And for your IN-FOR-MA-TION, he was there for me, too, when I was out of work, givin' me his last when I had nothin' and I know he really didn't have it either.

"Ughhhhhh!" Richelle threw the teddy bear across the room; its plastic eye hit the wall and made a loud clack.

It's probably broken or at least cracked, she thought. *Okay, I'm really goin' crazy, I can't even have a conversation with an inanimate object and not have it come down on me like my family does. I want to relax and not have to defend my relationship or my actions to anybody. I'm a grown woman! I'm twenty-nine years old and I pay my own bills and my own way in life; I shouldn't have to answer to nobody!*

I love my man, period. No, I'm not happy with the pace of our relationship at this time. If I had my way, we would've been married on New Year's Eve. I've always thought that would be a romantic thing to do. A candle-light ceremony, small and intimate, with only our closest friends and loved ones attendin', completin' our vows and being pronounced husband and wife at the stroke of midnight, bringin' in a new year with a new life together...

But it's the middle of July right now, so even that dream can't come true for another five months!

Richelle glanced at her watch and realized that Raymond would be at her place within ten minutes. "I told him last night that we should have a face-to-face conversation so that we could possibly come to some sort of compromise about our relationship. I better get up and wash my face and fix my hair!

"Can't be lookin' crazy or have any tear stains and puffy eyes when he sees me," she said to her teddy bear, which was upside down in the corner of her room, staring blankly back at her with one cracked plastic eye.

After washing her face, Richelle stared at herself in the bathroom mirror, examining her light brown eyes, checking for any signs that she had been crying. "You look good, girl," she told herself. "You just got your hair cut and dyed honey blonde – it really brings out your eyes and golden skin tone. Y*ou* are Ms. IT! Shoot, Ray better get it together. You are too fine to wait forever!" Richelle smiled as she left the bathroom and headed toward the kitchen.

In the kitchen, Richelle frantically rushed around, warming up the leftover food she had cooked the night before. Raymond was always hungry when he arrived at her place after the long two-hour drive and she wanted to have his plate ready for him when he arrived. "Lord, touch my tongue and guide my words as I express my feelings and thoughts to Raymond. Amen." she prayed.

The phone rang and Richelle rushed over to answer it. She thought it might have been Raymond calling on his cell phone. When she looked at the caller ID and saw her parents' home phone number, she said, "Oh, no. Not now, Momma. I know

Mickey must've called you and I ain't tryin' to hear it!"

She walked away from the still ringing phone to continue the preparations. "Voice mail is a great thing!" she giggled.

As soon as she got the plate out of the microwave, there was a knock at the door. *He's here,* she thought. *Okay, stay calm and open-minded and* don't *get angry - whatever you do, don't get angry. We don't need another shouting match.*

Richelle looked through her peephole and saw that it was Raymond. She always loved seeing his gorgeous caramel colored face. Richelle opened the door for Raymond, who was smiling like a Cheshire cat, showing off his perfect teeth and deep dimples. *I guess he must be glad to see me. I wonder if he forgot about all of the ugly things that I said last night?* she wondered as she stood on her tiptoes to give him a hug and then let him in the door.

"Hey, Baby," Raymond said as he hugged Richelle with one arm. When he stepped in the door, he pulled a dozen pink roses from behind his back and handed them to her, never losing the Cheshire-cat smile. "You look good. I like what you did with your hair. It looks nice short." Raymond said, as he looked her over. "Hmmm, Shelly, somethin' else besides you smells good in here. What'd you cook?" he asked as he strolled into the kitchen and glanced at his plate.

Richelle was totally taken back - not sure how to respond – and was quite unsure of what was going on. *And just why is he in such a good mood? Usually he's tired and sluggish when he gets here.*

"Well, last night I cooked some chicken parmesan, and I know how much you like it so, I heated some up for you," she answered Ray as she hugged his broad frame from behind. "I'm glad you made it here safely. Thank you for the roses; I think they're beautiful."

They kissed briefly before Ray sat down to eat.

"As always, Baby, this is good. Thank you for havin' it ready for me when I got here. You are so sweet, and always lookin' out for me!" Ray said with a mouth full of food.

"No problem. You're quite welcome," Richelle answered as she tried to spend some of her nervous energy by arranging the roses in a vase and picking up around her condo. She straightened the pillows on the couch, over-watered the plants, washed out a water glass that she had used earlier, and picked lint out of the carpet while Raymond ate his food.

"What're you all nervous for, girl?" Raymond asked her after she had gathered up about two handfuls of carpet lint. "You gon' make a bald spot in the carpet doin' that," he joked, looking at her with a raised eyebrow.

Richelle kept her eyes on the carpet and answered, "I ain't nervous. I'm fine. You need some more to drink?"

"Yeah, thanks. You know you make the "bomb" Kool-Aid!" he answered with a smile.

Richelle got up and poured Raymond some more Kool-Aid and then took his empty plate.

"Thanks again, Baby. That was delicious. Can I take this in the livin' room? I wanted to finish our discussion from last night." Ray asked as she handed him the refilled cup.

I should say, "no." He knows that I don't like nobody drinkin' in my livin' room! Richelle thought. She noticed that Ray was halfway into the living room anyway; so she decided that it was a statement and not an actual question.

"Sure," she said with a slight attitude. Richelle figured that either Raymond didn't hear her tone or chose to ignore it; either way he sat down on the couch and sipped his drink between his smiles.

Okay, after the past of hour that I've had, if he doesn't wipe that stupid smile off his face and tell me what there is to be so happy about, I think I'm going to scream! she thought, all the while looking calm on the outside, with a small smile.

"Okay, was it just a wonderful drive out here or what? You're smilin' like you've just won a million dollars."

Ray stopped smiling, cocked his head to the side and

looked at her with squinted eyes.

"Can't I just be happy to see my beautiful girlfriend? Hmph, anyway…I spent all of the drive here thinkin' about the conversations that we've had over the past few days. Seems like we can't reach middle ground regardin' our relationship. I've spent a lot of time thinkin' about what you've said and how you feel. I know how I feel and I know how I want to handle this between us…"

Richelle took a deep breath and thought, *Here we go girl. You've pushed him too far this time! He's come all the way out here just to break up with you and he's smilin' so much because he has lost his mind. Or maybe he feels relief, like a load has been lifted off of him since he has decided to get rid of you! Lord knows, if I lose this man behind listenin' to my family, we gon' be on the news: "Young African-American woman kills all of her female family members for giving her 'jacked up' advice about her love life, witnesses say. She lost her man and her mind. Story at eleven."*

All the time Richelle was daydreaming, Raymond was still talking.

"…and like I've told you many times, you know that I've dreamt of how I want to propose to my wife-to-be. I want to surprise her, at the moment when she least expects it, I want to show her how much I love her and care for her. Richelle, I love you very much, more than any woman that I've ever been with. You're so special to me and I don't think that you truly know just how special you are. It really frustrates me when you give me this funky attitude that makes me think that since we ain't married yet, you think that I don't care about you.

"I know your family is on your back, and I'm sorry that you let them in our business like that. I don't appreciate the extra pressure that they put on us. We're both under pressure to spend the rest of our lives the way other people see fit, and I don't think it's fair. Do you?" Raymond paused and looked at Richelle.

"No," she answered with her eyes downcast, staring at the

carpet and trying to brace herself emotionally for the imminent breakup.

He touched her chin and slowly lifted her head so that they were looking at each other eye-to-eye as he continued. "I don't take kindly to other people tellin' me how to live my life, and you already know that I'm a private person, not likin' my business in the streets. I've never liked people in my business and I've really had to think about that. Wonderin' if I could live a life with you being ruled by your family and what they think—"

"It doesn't have to be that way!" Richelle blurted out. "I've been keepin' them out of our business. I'm a grown woman and can think for myself. If I truly listened to them, I would've broken up with you a long time ago!"

Oh, Lord, help me through this! she prayed.

Raymond took a sip of his drink and shifted positions on the couch. He grabbed her hand and firmly held it within his own. "I know, Baby. I know. That's one of the things I love about you; you're very strong willed and independent. I think that if we're growin' together and workin' toward marriage, we should be each other's best friend and talk out our differences between ourselves. Not everyone has our best interests at heart. The devil can use any and everyone, and I don't want to lose you or this good thing we have together."

Aha! So he still thinks we have a good thing! Thank you, Lord. All is not lost! Richelle breathed a sigh of relief.

Uh, where's he goin'? Richelle wondered as Raymond got up abruptly and took his glass with him. He got up so fast, she thought that he had to use the bathroom and was surprised to see him go into the kitchen instead. He came back into the room with a strange look on his face that she couldn't quite read, and it made her nervous. *Guess I relaxed too soon.*

"Richelle, you have no clue as to how much I love you, how I only want what God wants for you, which is your ultimate best. And, to be truthful, I don't know if I can give it to you…" Raymond bent down in front of Richelle with tears in his eyes.

Richelle's eyes began to tear up as well as she thought, *Oh, okay. Here it goes. The "you're too good for me" speech that's supposed to make me feel as if his dumpin' me is the right thing to do and in my best interests, when the truth of it all is, him being a coward and leavin' me so that he doesn't have to marry me!*

"...but I want to and am willin' to try." Raymond pulled a small black box from his pocket and opened it to show Richelle a beautiful platinum and diamond engagement ring. Her jaw dropped; the ring was more gorgeous than she could have ever imagined. "OH MY GOD!" Richelle gasped as tears streamed from her eyes.

"Richelle Jackson, will you marry me?" Raymond asked. Richelle could barely stop crying to answer.

Smiling and crying she said, "Yes! Yes, Raymond Craig, I will marry you!"

Raymond smiled another Cheshire-cat smile and kissed her.

As she kissed him back, she prayed to God, *Thank you, Lord. THANK YOU, THANK YOU, THANK YOU! You came through for me again. Patience paid off and You have given me the man that I want, the way that I want him. Sorry for gettin' angry, impatient, and discouraged at times, and for listenin' to other voices. Shoot, they didn't know what they were talkin' about! All in my business, tryin' to tell me what to do, when all the while, You had it all under control! THANK YOU, THANK YOU, THANK YOU!*

Raymond got up off his knees and walked to the bathroom to get a damp towel to wipe her face. Richelle figured that he was still grinning from ear to ear because his mission had been accomplished, he had definitely surprised her. As he passed her bedroom, he spotted the teddy bear with the cracked eye in the corner and asked, "What happened to the bear?"

Richelle just laughed and replied, "Oh, nothin'."

DO YOU KNOW WHAT I DID?

"Aghhhhhh!" Iris misstepped and tripped on the curb. As she saw the gray slab of sidewalk coming closer and closer, she threw herself to the right to break her fall and hopefully avoid any scarring to her face. "This is not going to be my day. Maybe this is a sign that I shouldn't be out here," she said as she dusted off her clothing and picked up her picket sign.

Nope, that's just what happens when you aren't watching where you're going! Did you have a nice trip? asked a giggling voice inside her head.

This was Iris's first time picketing an abortion clinic, and she felt uneasy. Her mentor from church, Stacy, had convinced her to come out and support a "worthy" cause.

"We may even save the life of a child today!" she exclaimed. Stacy was always zealous over anything that she deemed as a "moral and worthy" cause. She was the stereotypical "blonde"; she was blonde, blue-eyed, and slightly air-headed. Her excitement level was always highly contagious, and before Iris knew it, Stacy had her committed to picketing and out on the front lines before she could give the idea another thought. Now, in the midday sun, as she watched young women try to walk through the doors of the clinic, some disturbed by the photos on the picket signs and others being harassed by the picketers, Iris decided that this was *definitely* a bad idea. Her head began to ache as her heart melted within her. Her feelings of uneasiness turned into full-blown guilt. She felt like a hypocrite, the biggest hypocrite in the world. Here she was picketing, trying to prevent these young women from having an abortion, and she hadn't even prevented herself from having one. As a matter of fact, she had cursed the picketers so badly on the day of her appointment that they tried to get physically violent with her. Who was she to think that she had a right to say anything?

Iris spotted a young woman trying to pass the picketers who reminded her of herself. The young woman was fair-skinned, tall, and lean with huge dark brown eyes that looked as if they were filled with uncertainty. *Yeah, she looks a lot like me*, Iris thought.

As she remembered her own abortion, Iris recalled how she hadn't wanted to be pregnant or attached to Charles forever. She remembered feeling scared, lost, and alone. She wondered if her "look-a-like" was feeling the same way that she had felt.

Your situation was totally different from that girl that you see there, her self-righteous inner voice, Anna, told her. *She's just some loose girl who is probably a habitual aborter, using it as a method of birth control. You, on the other hand, had a special situation, a good reason for doing what you did. There would have been two lives taken instead of one if you had not had that abortion. You, my dear, Iris saved a life.*

Whenever she was feeling stressed, Iris liked listening to Anna. Anna was so rational, and always right - at least that's what Anna would tell Iris. When she listened to Anna, Iris felt superior, as if she was better than everyone else in the world. Anna justified every decision – good and bad – that Iris had ever made. Let Anna tell it, Iris was never guilty of anything. But even after hearing Anna's voice, Iris felt torn between her moral code of letting others choose their own direction, her personal desire to stop the young woman that she saw from making the same mistake that she had made, and the anguish from her own soul, condemning her past actions.

She's still a murderer and a hypocrite, no matter how you try to spin it, Anna! There's no amount of self-righteous propaganda that you can brainwash her with that will change the facts! retorted an angry matronly voice. It was one of Iris's other voices, Carmen.

Whenever Iris heard Anna's voice, she knew that Carmen was sure to follow. The two voices were always at odds and

Carmen always had something negative to say. She was constantly judging and condemning Iris. Hearing Carmen's voice had a way of making Iris feel as if *everything* in the whole world was her fault, and Carmen consistently played on the fact that Iris was overly concerned with what other people thought of her.

Iris closed her eyes to hold back her tears as she remembered not wanting to shame her parents - who thought that she was still virgin - or her church family with the scandal of her being pregnant. *How would they react now if they knew what I have done? What would they have to say?* she wondered.

They would say the exact same thing that I'm saying; you are going to burn in Hell for what you did! screamed Carmen.

As Anna and Carmen waged their familiar battle inside of her mind, Iris's headache grew worse. She didn't even realize that she was sitting down on the curb with her hands to her temples until she heard Stacy asking her a question.

"Are you all right?" Stacy asked. "Do you need an aspirin? You look like you don't feel too good!" As Stacy reached into her purse for a pill bottle, Iris reached up and grabbed her hand to stop her.

"No, thanks. I'm fine. Just give me a minute, okay? You know that I have a weak stomach, and some of the pictures on the signs are kinda gross." Iris smiled weakly, hoping to give Stacy the impression that she was okay.

"Hee hee," Stacy giggled. "They're supposed to be gross! We are trying to shock and scare, remember? We want these women to know that what they are trying to do is horrible. We want them to do the right thing -give life, not cause death!"

Iris didn't respond to Stacy, she just continued to rub her fingers over her temples, hoping that Stacy would take the hint and go away.

"Okay, well, I'll be back to check on you," Stacy said as she walked away toting a huge sign with a gruesome photo of a bloody aborted fetus.

Looking at the pictures on the signs did make my stomach queasy, Iris told herself as she justified the half-truth that she had just told Stacy. Reminded of how sensitive she is, Iris told herself that she should have known that she wouldn't have been able to live with the decision to terminate her pregnancy, and that she *really* should have known better than to come out to the picket line.

Glad she's gone, huh? asked the giggly voice in Iris's head. It was Shantelle. She, too, came around when Iris was under stress and she usually came with jokes. Even though her comments were filled with silly remarks and sarcasm, Shantelle's voice helped Iris to laugh when she felt like crying.

With the three voices chatting away inside of her head - all at the same time - Iris couldn't think straight.

"If I needed to hear any of my voices right now, I would like to hear from Tawnie," Iris moaned as the pain inside of her head increased.

You rang, love? Iris smiled at the sound of the comforting Southern twang. It was Tawnie, her favorite voice. To Iris, Tawnie was the voice of comfort. Tawnie's voice got her through the nervous breakdown that she had had after the abortion. Tawnie was the voice of love, compassion, patience, and persistence; she never gave up, even when the other voices were predicting Iris's demise. She talked Iris right out of the dark abyss of mental and emotional instability and brought her back into reality.

"I need to know which one of you told me that it was okay to have the abortion, anyway?" Iris asked her group of mental comrades. "You guys all know that it went against everything that I believe in."

Shantelle piped up. *Oh, oh, I know! It was Anna! She said that since you were in your second year of law school, you didn't need a baby. She said you had a great career ahead of you and that you shouldn't spoil it. She even told you not to tell Charles about the baby. Said he'd only try to stop you. Yep, that's exactly what she said!*

That's enough, you goofy idiot! Anna yelled. *I told her to do what was right! Everything would have been fine if Carmen hadn't opened her big mouth. I had Iris convinced that I was right; that it was the best thing for her, and that it was a decision that she could live with. She didn't want the baby, anyway!*

But, oh, no! Carmen had to start in with her gibberish about the baby being a life and that abortion was murder! She confused the poor child and allowed her to hear Laura!

Oh no, you don't, Anna! Don't you start blaming me! Laura was not my doing! I was trying to spare Iris from sinning against God, the child, and herself. It was, is, and will always *be a sin!* Carmen said. *She was as wrong as two left feet, and now she is suffering for it. And I for one am glad, because she deserves it! I told her this would happen. I told her so!*

Please, you two! pleaded Tawnie in an agitated voice. *Don't ya'll think that ya'll have done enough? I think that ya'll both are to blame. You should be ashamed! Ya'll take Iris from one extreme to the next and then ya'll wonder why Laura came? Can't ya'll just let Iris be? Truth be told, yeah, she had an abortion. But it's in the past, it happened, and it's over. Don't ya'll realize that Laura only came because Iris was overwhelmed with guilt? If ya'll two don't stop this bickerin', ya'll will make things much worse in here. Iris can't take all of this...*

I liked Laura! Shantelle interrupted with a singsong voice.
Shut UP! yelled the other three voices in unison.

"I didn't like Laura," mumbled Iris. Laura's voice came from the dark abyss and Iris knew it to be the voice of death and doom, the voice that had planted the suicidal thoughts in her head. Laura's voice was the one that Iris was listening to as she contemplated killing herself so that no one would ever know about the baby and she wouldn't have to have an abortion.

It was Laura who kept her mentally confined and emotionally cold during the abortion procedure, the voice that convinced Iris that it would be better to bleed to death than to seek medical help when she started to hemorrhage after the abortion.

All of the other voices feared Laura because she meant to destroy Iris and thereby destroy them all. But for now, Laura was dormant, somewhere in the recesses of Iris's mind. And all of them, including Iris, hoped that she stayed there.

"Hey, Iris, are you feeling any better?" Iris looked up to see Stacy standing over her with a look of motherly concern. "I know that this is your first time out here, seeing the pictures and being around this type of stuff. Girl, forgive me if I was being a bit insensitive toward you, especially since you are a 'newbie'." Stacy smiled and offered her hand to help Iris up off the curb.

"It's all right, Stacy. It's just... I have no business being here and I think that coming out today was a bad idea..."

No, girlie, I think that you fit right in! You should come out every day! interrupted Shantelle with a silly high-pitched giggle.

"...I really don't feel comfortable, and I don't think that I should be out here trying to dictate to these women what they should or shouldn't do..."

That's the truth! You're no better than them, you no-good hypocrite! Carmen snapped.

Just stop it, Carmen! Iris repented a long time ago. Have ya ever heard of the word "forgiveness"? For all of your talk about God, you've forgotten that He still loves this girl. Ya need to stop bein' so judgmental and just let it go so that Iris can let it go! exclaimed an exasperated Tawnie.

"...with their bodies..." Iris tried to finish her sentence, but pain interrupted her thoughts. She abruptly stopped talking and grabbed her forehead as she tried to contain the mounting pain and quiet the voices.

Stacy sat down next to her on the curb.

"*Okay*, you're starting to scare me. Should I take you home so that you can get some rest? Are you *sure* that you're okay?" Stacy asked.

Iris slowly shook her head, while she held her forehead

within the palm of her hand, determined to keep her head from exploding under the pressure of the extreme stress headache.

"Please don't let me black out, God," Iris softly prayed.

"Look Stacy, I'm not who you think I am. I'm not some goodie two-shoes, and I will never qualify as being perfect..." Iris started. "Trust me, I'm not who you think I am. You have no clue about what I have done!" Iris said as she burst into tears. Stacy put her arm around Iris's shoulder to try to comfort her.

"Iris, what's wrong? What're you talking about? I know that no one is perfect, and I want you to know that I'm here for you, and you can tell me *anything*."

As Iris opened her mouth to finish telling Stacy her secret, she felt a searing pain inside of her head, as if she had been stabbed with a burning knife. All of a sudden, in the midst of the terrible pain, she could hear all of the voices in her head yelling and screaming. Iris knew that something was dreadfully wrong.

"Oh, no!" Shantelle cried. *She's coming! Laura is coming! Anna, try to stop her!"*

"You know that Anna can't stop her any more than any of us can," sighed Carmen.

"I told ya'll this was too much for Iris; that's why Laura's comin'. Truthfully, this is too much for me to try to deal with again. Maybe we should just step aside; it's probably for the best..." Tawnie said as she resigned, accepting defeat.

"Glad to know that everyone knows why I'm here," interrupted Laura. *"I've been sitting back, listening, patiently waiting for my time to return. I knew that it would come. Iris is just too torn up inside over the abortion. And with you two, Anna and Carmen, arguing and playing a game of moral tug-of-war on the girl's mind, you made quite the ripe and fertile soil for my return. You might as well have rolled out the red carpet for me,"* gloated Laura. *"Rest assured ladies, you're no longer needed; I can take it from here."*

The other voices quickly faded into the recesses of Iris's mind as Laura took control.

Iris? Iiiirrrisss? I know that you can hear me, girl. What's wrong, sweetie? Not feeling too well? Oh, that's too bad. Let me see if I can figure out what's been going on here. I know! You're remembering the abortion. Hahahaha! It's a little late, girlfriend, to start trippin' off of what you did now. But I guess you feel the need to unburden your soul, thinking that if you tell this Stacy chick about your secret, that all of the guilt will go away. Sorry, honey, confession ain't good for the soul this *time!*

Hey, I've got an idea! Since you're already strolling down memory lane and reliving the past, let's play "Remember when." Then you can really have something to tell!

"No!" Iris yelled.

"No? Iris, don't you trust me?" Stacy asked in disbelief.

Iris didn't answer Stacy because she could no longer hear Stacy. The only voice that she could hear was Laura's.

Hey, Iris, you wanna tell Stacy about how you asked to see the ultrasound picture of the baby before the abortion? Truthfully, you had me a bit nervous when you did that. I thought if you saw the baby, you would change your mind. But I underestimated the hold that I had on you, because even after seeing the picture, you still went through with it. You saw *the child within your womb and you still chose to kill it. Go on and tell Stacy just how heartless you are!*

Or, better yet, tell her what happened when the nurse gave you the IV of anesthesia. Remember? You had the nerve *to ask her when it would take effect! What made you ask that? Did you think to ask if it numbed the baby so that it wouldn't feel the pain that accompanied being torn to pieces by a high-powered vacuum? I seriously doubt it.*

Can you just imagine the kind of pain that poor baby felt? I bet Stacy could show you some pictures and tell you all about the torture that the fetuses go through. Iris, come on girl, you have got *to remember the sounds of the machine, the loud whirring noise. You do, don't you? Make sure that you describe that to Stacy, too, since you want to tell something!*

And when she asks you what were you thinking and why did you do it, make sure that you're honest. Don't even try to lie; we both know that you weren't thinking of the life that was leaving your body. Nope, you know you weren't, 'cause all you were thinking about was yourself, just being selfish! You know what, though? I loved it! Afterward, you went right into the recovery room, but nobody told you that you would never recover, did they?

Your body has healed, but as we both know, your mind hasn't. And it never will, as long as I have a say. So, Iris, instead of telling Stacy your secret, you should just come on back with me. You know that the darkness was safe; you know that there was comfort there. Just stop trying to fight it and come back to where people like you - horrible baby killers - belong. Come on...that's right Iris, come on back into the darkness...

As Iris slipped from consciousness, she barely heard Stacy screaming for someone to call 911. She hoped that the paramedics would be too late. Iris thought that she was dying and she was all right with the idea. She would no longer have to share or live with her secret. Iris was content knowing that only she and God knew of all of the things that she had done in her lifetime, and felt that it was best if it stayed that way. With the hope that she would talk to Him soon, she decided that if He didn't bring up any of her transgressions when she got there, she wouldn't either.

"I just hope I'm forgiven," were the last words that Iris mumbled as she was being placed into the ambulance by the emergency medics. As darkness engulfed her, Iris heard a small still voice - that she believed to be the voice of God - answer her and say, "Yes, my child, you are loved and forgiven."

♀ ♀

PART III

~ GROWING OLD

I was once young
But now I'm old
When I die
I don't want all
My secrets told!

♀ ♀

♀ THE END OF A JOURNEY ♀

The sun couldn't break the chill that was in the air on the Tuesday morning of her funeral. Her friends and loved ones were all bundled up as they shuffled their way among the narrowly spaced church pews. They were all saddened at the sight of the closed pink casket that was covered with large pink and white roses. There was a poster-sized portrait of the smiling elderly African-American woman with a rosy complexion and deep gray eyes next to the casket in which she was laid.

The church was filled with the ripe floral scents from the many different funeral sprays mingled with the scent of burning candles. The candelabras held a total of eighty-three candles - one for each year of her life - and added a peaceful and cozy touch to the dimly lit auditorium. As the ushers seated the last of the guests, the close friends and family of the deceased began to slowly make their way to the front of the church to take their seats in the designated pews. They were all wearing black with a single pink carnation pinned to their lapels, courtesy of the church's bereavement committee.

Everyone knew how much she loved the color pink. She loved people too, especially children. It was obvious by the way the small church was packed, filled with two and three generations of lives that she had touched in some form or fashion. In contrast to the outdoor weather, the auditorium was a bit warm. The local funeral home fans started to move the air around heavily perfumed women, as they tried to cool down and coats were shed, as many mourners made themselves comfortable.

A young man who bore a striking resemblance to the woman in the portrait left his seat in the front pew and stepped up to the pulpit to open the service. Chance, her eldest grandson, adjusted his tie and jacket, then led the mourners in the opening prayer.

"Dear Lord, our Heavenly Father, we have come to you today as we celebrate the home-going of my beloved grandmother, Aries Jaye Jowell, best known by all who loved her as Momma Jowell. You know, Lord, that death has a devastating effect on the soul of man. Please touch our grieving hearts, oh Lord, and keep us mindful that she is in a better place, singing with the angels next to Your throne.

"She died the way that she always wanted to – peacefully, in her sleep. We thank You for Your mercy, Lord, and for not allowing her to suffer. Please bless our family, that we may grow closer together during this time of bereavement, and that we may be as You would have us to be in Your sight. In Your Son Jesus' name we do pray, Amen."

The audience repeated "Amen" in unison as Chance stepped down to take his seat.

Following the prayer, a plump young woman stepped up to the pulpit to sing a solo of "Peace in the Valley." Chyna Murphy was the regular soloist at all of the weddings and funerals held at Beaux Street. As her soulful alto voice filled the room, the words of the song brought tears to everyone's eyes. It was Momma Jowell's favorite song and Chyna was singing it with many smooth runs and riffs, showing off all of the vocal training that she received from her beloved mentor, Momma Jowell. Her acappella singing was so touching that no one seemed to mind that she was overextending each verse of the song with her ad-libs.

Before Chyna finished her solo, Art, Aries's youngest son, joined her in the pulpit and blended his strong tenor voice into the song. Their duet evoked heavy sobs and wailing throughout the audience. No one was able to hold their composure; tissues were being passed, fans fluttered at high speeds, and all thoughts were on how Momma Jowell would have loved to hear this kind of singing.

When the duet was finished, Chyna hugged Art and headed to her seat toward the back of the church. She smiled as she graciously accepted all of the whispered compliments and comments that she heard as she passed the mourners in the pews.

Art remained in the pulpit, sobbing softly. As he wiped away his tears and regained his composure, he began to speak to the audience. "I know that we are all touched by the loss of my dear mother, but let us now lift up our voices and sing with all of the heart and soul that she would sing with, if she were here with us right now. I don't want you to just sing…I want you all to *sang*!"

Many in the audience - especially the choir members - smiled, and others chuckled as Art imitated his mother. Aries had led the church choir for fifteen years, and would always let the group know before every performance that she didn't want to hear no singing, she wanted them to get out there and *sang*.

Art led four upbeat hymns and lightened the moods of many in the audience. Everyone sang from the heart, and not one person shed a single tear during the song service. At the end of the last hymn, Art announced that Jeri Mae Hamilton - a dear friend of the family - would give the eulogy. Art left the pulpit and assisted Jeri Mae past a brigade of flower sprays, up the few steps to the pulpit, and then led the little old woman over to the microphone. He bent over and gave her a kiss on the cheek before he went to take his seat.

Jeri Mae and Aries had been childhood friends. They grew up together in the same neighborhood, sharing toys, clothes, and families. Even though they weren't blood related, they had become extended family. As they grew older and life pulled them in separate directions, they eventually grew apart from each other, but they never lost contact or the love that they had for one another. They were "sisters" and they were best friends.

Jeri Mae adjusted her bifocals and stared at the envelope that she held in her left hand. When she looked back up at the crowd, she felt a growing lump in her throat, an unwelcome companion to her already shaking knees. Crowds had always made her nervous. Beside the fact that she had never given a eulogy before, Jeri Mae had never even *heard* of anyone doing what Aries had asked her to do two years prior to her death.

"Aries always wanted to be different; she always had to steal the show," Jeri Mae muttered to herself. She lowered the microphone so that it was just inches from her face. With her voice wavering with more fear than sorrow, she addressed the crowd.

"I must tell ya'll that I'm sad to be here, but I'm in front of ya today, to talk about my best friend, Aries Jaye Jowell. Jayia, Arthur, Robert, Carly, ya'll know I loved your momma, and I love you kids like ya'll my own. I remember when each of you was born, and I was there to see it, too! Precious little babies ya'll were! Ya'll know, I couldn't never have no children of my own. Bad luck, I guess. I forget what the doctor said was wrong with me…but, oh well.

"Yeah, I'm gon' miss yo' old momma. Yes, indeedy. I remember when we were younger. Used to do some wild and crazy things. Ol' Jeri Mae and Aries Jaye, hmph, we were too much! Yo' momma sho' was a hot mama, ha, ha! But, yeah, she was a sister to me, and as heartbroken as I am that she's gone, I'm honored that she asked me to eulogize her during her home-goin' celebration.

"But, bein' Aries, she didn't feel that any words that I could come up with would be good enough. She wanted to talk to ya'll about herself today. She was always like that, thinkin' I'm slow and stupid. I ain't never been neither! She got on my last nerve with that! Matter of fact, I think she owed me twenty dollars! Jayia, I want the money that yo' momma owed me from *you* before I leave!"

The entire auditorium was hushed. The group of mourners was completely silent. The hand-held fans suddenly stopped moving and it seemed as if no one was breathing. You could have heard a pin drop. Jeri Mae's outburst had startled everyone; no one could believe that she had just said some of the things that she had said about Momma Jowell. Friends and family members looked at each other with confusion. Had the shock of Aries's death made Jeri Mae slip over the *edge*? Her mind had been slipping over the past years, making her already cantankerous mood and loose tongue worse than they had ever been. Everyone in the audience wondered if the old woman had finally lost "it".

Shaunice whispered to her husband Chance, "I told you that crazy old bat has Alzheimer's!"

Chance just shifted in his seat while he dabbed beads of sweat off his forehead; his eyes never left Jeri Mae. Jeri Mae cleared her throat to break the uncomfortable silence and continued on.

"Don't think I don't know ya'll think I'm crazy. I know you don't understand what I'm tryin' to say. That old woman had to be the star once again! Not that she wasn't gon' be the star at her own funeral! Hmph, Ms. Aries wrote her *own* eulogy that she wanted me to read. I have it right here in my hand."

She held up the envelope to show it to the audience. "Now, I'm gon' read this, so listen up and bear with me. I haven't opened it since she gave it to me; the words that you'll hear are all hers. She wanted her day to be all about her, from beginning to end…I guess she forgot that when it's your *own* funeral, it's usually all about you anyway!"

Jeri Mae rolled her eyes as she opened the envelope. She carefully unfolded the letter and stared at Aries' calligraphic handwriting. As she hesitated, she could hear Aries's voice inside of her head yelling, "Gon' 'head and read it, girl! It won't bite!"

Jeri Mae sighed long, hard, and a bit too loud into the microphone as she began reading.

"I was just sittin' here thinkin' to myself," Aries's eulogy began, *"who better to talk about me and my life than me? Ha, nobody! I know me better than all ya'll put together. I've also been to enough funerals to know that ya'll will take at least an hour with your personal remarks about*

*me, that're supposed to be limited to two
minutes. But some of ya'll will take at least five
minutes, goin' on and on about what you knew
and what you thought you knew about me. Some
of ya'll will feel the need to be in the spotlight,
singin' solos - some off-key - and dedicatin' 'em
to me. I even bet that there are folks here who I
didn't like and who sho' nuff didn't like me.
Before I go any further, can you please kick them
fake folks out?*

A couple of people in the audience considered going up to
the pulpit and throwing Jeri Mae out the door after hearing
Momma Jowell's request. Some people snickered, while others
laughed out loud, remembering Momma Jowell's sense of humor
and her way of seeing things. She was truly something else. Her
personality was coming back through those words - her words -
and it felt like she was still there with them in the church, speaking
her mind and "telling it like it is."

*To tell ya'll the truth, with all that will be said
here today, I'm sure it will be a beautiful picture
of my life. But, since this is my day, my home-
goin' celebration, and I don't feel like gettin' up
from this pretty and comfortable coffin that ya'll
have me layin' in, I've left with you what I wanted
you to hear about me and my life. Those who
knew me know I wasn't much on tellin' my
business, but I couldn't stand it when somebody
else was tryin' to tell my business, especially
when they got it wrong.*

Jeri Mae stopped reading and asked one of the children on
the front pew to get her some water. Art's daughter, Alicia, went
back into the fellowship hall to grant Jeri Mae's request. When

she looked out over the crowd, Jeri Mae saw many different facial expressions. Some showed sadness, others revealed piqued curiosity, and some just looked downright annoyed, anxious for her to keep reading so that they could hear what the woman they affectionately knew as Momma Jowell had to say.

Jeri Mae decided to continue reading in spite of the fact that her water had not arrived. She figured she'd just deal with the dry mouth for a little while longer and not cause the crowd to turn into an impatient angry mob.

> *I bet ya'll look so nice today, probably dressed in your Sunday best, and I know there ain't no red or teary eyes showin'. Plenty of ya'll probably got on them ol' ugly dark sunglasses that I always hated. Ain't nothin' to be ashamed of showin' emotion. I bet some of you are just a-cryin'. Oh, my sweet babies, ain't nothin' wrong with that, either; just make sure you got some tissue. I don't want none of ya'll to be embarrassed, walkin' around with boogas hangin' from your noses, 'cause you know ain't nobody gon' tell you! They just gon' keep on talkin' to you like ain't nothin' wrong.*

Laughter erupted in the audience and many women simultaneously dug into their purses, pulling out mirrored compacts and tissue wads. Everyone was sniffling and touching their noses doing "booga checks." A few mourners even left out to go to the restroom.

> *Okay, okay, enough of my jokes. I'm sure that I've made the mood a bit lighter in here. I'll finish up so that ya'll can get on with livin'.*
> *Most of you here today never saw me without a smile. A lot of people thought that I was a crazy*

woman. They labeled me "crazy" for so many different reasons. I laughed at my own jokes, especially when nobody else got the punch line. I believed in what most people considered to be unbelievable. I loved when others thought it wasn't possible or profitable - even when I didn't wanna love, I still did.

I could look at life with rose-colored glasses one minute, and in the next, see life as a pile of sugar-coated dog mess. Strangely enough, I could be as optimistic as I could be pessimistic. I encouraged others to keep goin' and to follow their dreams, even when it seemed that all of the odds were against them. Why? 'Cause it was my gift, my purpose for bein' here on this earth. Yep, my gift from God and my gift to the world, I was sent to encourage and to reach people.

Don't get me wrong, now. I was no saint; I made plenty of mistakes and bad judgment calls within my lifetime. I tried to do a bit more good than evil so, Lord willin', I won't have no gate trouble on the other side. But keepin' it real, I've broken all Ten Commandments, some commandments more times over than others. Don't let my sweet face fool ya!

See today, I'm gon' tell it like it W-A-S. I always hated it when I'd go to a funeral of the biggest devil in the world and all some people wanted to do was to stand there and talk about how good *that person was. The preacher would actually stand up in the house of God and outright lie to make the family feel better!*

Shoot, they was related! The family knew the person wasn't about nothin' no way and they was probably glad *the no-good fool was finally gone! I*

*figured that folks tell all those lies 'cause it's
supposed to be impolite to talk bad about the
dead. Hmph! From what I know, it's a sin to lie.*

*Now, let's see. About my life...I didn't start out
with a silver spoon in my mouth, that's for sure. I
grew up poor, and everybody in the neighborhood
looked like me, Black. We lived in a community
where all of the Black folks owned their houses,
but not much more. I think it's safe to say that I
was raised in the ghetto. Nobody had any more
than the next person, and everybody was just
tryin' to survive.*

*I was blessed to have both of my parents in the
house. Mama and Daddy gave me a picture-
perfect example of what a lovin' relationship was
supposed to be like. Bein' I had two brothers and
three sisters, I developed a sharin' nature through
necessity. We lived in a small three-bedroom
frame house with one bathroom. It was crowded,
to say the least.*

*I can't say that I had too much of nothin' that I
could call my own growin' up. Bein' I was the
second to the youngest girl, everything was a
hand-me-down or had to be shared with
somebody else. That's why singin' was always an
important part of my life. My voice was my own,
and I could share it with others only when I
wanted to.*

*None of my siblings could sing, so when I
opened my mouth and sang, I became the center
of attention. Everybody always wondered and
admired how such a powerful voice could come
from somebody so tiny. I was always small for my
age, but I had big dreams for my life. I had*

dreams of bein' a big-time superstar and becomin' rich. There would be no more room and clothes sharin' for me once I made it big! I wanted to be successful and LIVE, not just survive. I had stars in my eyes and plans on having the Good Life.

I started to sing at local nightclubs when I turned sixteen, and was eventually discovered by Silas Thomas, a "big-city" agent who said that he could make me go places. I was so excited and green. He had me hooked when he said he was an agent from New York City. I just knew my dreams were about to come true.

Well, my dreams halfway came true. Silas booked me at nightclubs and other 'hole-in-the-wall' spots so I could get some exposure...well, that's what he told me. And of course, I believed him. I was young, cute, and petite and I had the voice of an angel; I gave all of the other local singers a run for their money! I was sure I was goin' places and I wanted to get there fast!

Silas promised to take me to New York, Los Angeles, and all of the other places I'd dreamed of. I was in love with Silas and in love with the new life that I thought awaited me. My dreams were finally comin' true...so I thought. But my dreams slowly unraveled with the discovery of each and every one of Silas's lies. I had my brief moment to move the crowd in those no-count nightclubs, but I never made it to the big time.

Bein' my heart had always been bigger than my head, I was in deep trouble before I knew what happened. I was slapped into a reality of findin' out that I was bigamously married to Silas, broke without a dollar to my name - because I let him handle all of the money that I earned - and I had a baby on the way.

I didn't know what to do. I was eighteen, heartbroken, and had no clue as to what kind of life I'd have for myself, let alone what kind of life I'd provide for the new life that was growin' inside me. But, I can say wakin' up, realizin' that I wasn't gon' be a star, but I was definitely gon' be a mother, it settled me. Made me reevaluate what I wanted out of life, what was truly important. I still wanted to succeed in life and I was determined not to let my circumstances define or defeat me. I knew that I had to change my definition of success, and I had to change my way of life.

My new way of livin' consisted of me, of course, turnin' to the Lord. I know that sounds pathetic, and it truly is pathetic how everybody turns to God once their own way of livin' don't work. We all can testify that God is good, and He did indeed bless me in many, many ways.

After the birth of my first son, Robert, I took a job cleanin' at the local hospital during the nights. That's where I met Maverick. He, too, was a janitor at the hospital, and helped me with a lot of my duties. Quiet as kept, that was his way of showin' his interest and courtin' me.

I couldn't believe it. In spite of all that I had been through, God had sent me a wonderful man who fell in love with me and my son. Maverick was the most handsome man I had ever seen in my life, and he was twice as good lookin' on the inside. I married him six months after we met.

Maverick Jowell, yes, Lawd, now that was a M-A-N! They don't make 'em like that no more, let me tell ya'! He came into my life when I was at my lowest point and supported me and my son, not only financially, but also mentally, emotionally, and spiritually as well. He showed me love in a whole new light and taught me that life could be just as wonderful when you made your own 'lights' and danced on your own 'stage' to your own unique melody. I look forward to seein' him in Heaven because he was truly my angel.

I was also blessed with four lovely children, Robert, Jayia, Carly and Arthur. My babies - no matter how old they are, they'll still be my babies - have brought more joy to my life than grief, and they gave me the opportunity to give love and get it mirrored right back. In raisin' my children, I learned dependence and independence, the necessity of love, and that I could give even when I thought I had nothin' left to offer.

Maverick and I tried to raise them in the Lord and I know that, when I too have gone on Home, they'll be just fine. Art, Jayia, Carly, and Robert, I know that all of you are probably listenin', and I just want you to know that I love you and am still with you in your hearts and minds. Be strong and rest in the assurance that I'm with God and Daddy now.

I can say that I'm very happy that I was blessed with a church home. It's important to be able to worship the Lord where you feel comfortable, where the doctrine is sound, and where you feel like you fit in. I gained a marvelous church family that I was more connected to than most of my own relatives. Shows that the blood of Christ is much thicker than any blood relationship. Beaux Street church of Christ, ya'll were a great source of love, comfort, and strength during my life, and I know ya'll will be blessed. Again, I want to say thank you for all that you did for me when my Maverick passed away, and I'm thankin' you for all that I know you're doin' right now for my children and other family members as they grieve over my home-goin'.

Overall, I had a life filled with love from family and friends alike. There were good days as well as bad. I struggled a lot, but I smiled a lot, too, even in the midst of my struggles. I can truly say that I've been blessed. I was successful in my life and I was sho'll nuff happy. And now, I'm at peace.

The words of advice that I want to leave with you are from the Word of God; forgive me for not quotin' exact scriptures but ya'll know it's in there somewhere between Genesis and Revelations. First of all, love God with all your heart and always keep Him first. Remember to treat people as you wanna be treated; ya'll reap what you sow. And another thing, make sure that you live. There are too many people walkin' around here existin' and survivin'. Very few of 'em are actually livin', takin' the time to enjoy life.

Most folks just give up, suck up the pain of life without searchin' for any happiness, and trudge along toward their graves. Life is a test. This ain't no practice test to jog your memory and get you ready for the real thing. There's nothin' to get ya'll warmed up; you just gotta hit the ground runnin'. Know that you playin' for keeps.

I know the road gets hard, but I've lived a long time, long enough to know that there's always sunshine after the rain. No matter how long it takes for the sun to shine, it'll shine again. Try to make decisions that you know you can live with, and accept responsibility for all of the decisions that you make.

Finally, be sure that you keep those that you love close to you, and don't be afraid to tell them that you love them while they can still hear you. Roses are always nice when you're alive to enjoy them, and so are the words "I love you."

Well, that's all I wanted to say. I'm sure ya'll still have your remarks. Keep it short and sweet for me, and I look forward to seein' ya'll again on the other side.

Until we meet again,
Momma Jowell.

Jeri Mae folded the letter and placed it back in the envelope. She didn't say any closing remarks - pleasing many in the audience - she just turned and left the podium, letter still in hand. Art assisted her back down the steps and seated her on the front pew. Jeri Mae wept softly as she remembered her friend, realizing that she was truly gone and how much she would miss her. Art's wife Tina consoled Jeri Mae and handed her tissues. Alicia was once again given the task of getting Jeri Mae some water.

The audience was quiet, and everyone seemed to be in a thoughtful mood, waiting to see what would happen next. This was *definitely* the most original funeral any of them had ever attended. Even in death, Momma Jowell "did it again." Surprisingly, no one came forth with any remarks; all were content with allowing Momma Jowell to speak for herself on her day.

The Beaux Street choir sang many of Momma Jowell's favorite Negro spirituals, just as she had arranged them, while the final viewing procession took place. Friends and loved ones paid their respects to the family and laid tokens of love in Momma Jowell's casket, ranging from poetry to flowers. Many mourners said goodbye with kisses and a few even took pictures of how peaceful she looked.

At the end of the procession, her children and grandchildren gathered around the open casket - hand in hand - to say their final good-bye. Many memories of the times that they each shared with Momma Jowell flashed through their minds -the food, the fun, and the fussing. Even though they still shed tears, all agreed that Momma Jowell was in a better place, and they were thankful for all of the life lessons that she had shared with them. As the casket closed and the pallbearers prepared to carry her out, they all pledged in their hearts to see her again...on the other side.

♀ <u>NOTE FROM THE AUTHOR</u> ♀

Now that you have finished my book,
I would love to hear from you!

Please send your comments to: **jayejcaldwell@yahoo.com**
Or, if you prefer, you can contact me through the publisher.
And again, thank you for supporting my work.

*When I am gone, I want to be remembered as one who
encouraged many, loved sincerely, and served diligently
using my God-given talents. I want to be known as one who
did all she could.*

J.J.C

Printed in the United States
25300LVS00001B/165